Hezekiah Butterworth

**The Pilot of the Mayflower**

A Tale of the Children of the Pilgrim Republic

Hezekiah Butterworth

**The Pilot of the Mayflower**
*A Tale of the Children of the Pilgrim Republic*

ISBN/EAN: 9783337088385

Printed in Europe, USA, Canada, Australia, Japan

Cover: Foto ©Andreas Hilbeck / pixelio.de

More available books at **www.hansebooks.com**

# THE PILOT OF THE MAYFLOWER

### A TALE OF THE CHILDREN
### OF THE PILGRIM REPUBLIC

# BY HEZEKIAH BUTTERWORTH

---

**Brother Jonathan;** OR, THE ALARM POST IN THE
CEDARS. A Tale of Early Connecticut. Illustrated.

**In the Days of Jefferson;** OR, THE SIX GOLDEN
HORSESHOES. Illustrated by F. T. Merrill and Others.

**The Story of Magellan.** A Tale of the Discovery
of the Philippines. Illustrated by F. T. Merrill.

**The Treasure Ship.** A Story of Sir William Phipps
and the Inter-Charter Period in Massachusetts. Illustrated by B. West Clinedinst and Others.

**The Pilot of the Mayflower.** Illustrated.

**True to His Home.** A Tale of the Boyhood of Frank-
lin. Illustrated by H. Winthrop Peirce.

**The Wampum Belt;** OR, THE FAIREST PAGE OF
HISTORY. A Tale of William Penn's Treaty with
the Indians. With 6 full-page Illustrations.

**The Patriot Schoolmaster.** A Tale of the Minute-
men and the Sons of Liberty. With 6 full-page Illustrations by H. Winthrop Peirce.

**In the Boyhood of Lincoln.** A Story of the Black
Hawk War and the Tunker Schoolmaster. With 12
Illustrations and colored Frontispiece.

**The Boys of Greenway Court.** A Story of the
Early Years of Washington. Illustrated.

**The Log School-House on the Columbia.** Illustrated by J. Carter Beard, E. J. Austen, and Others.

---

D. APPLETON AND COMPANY, NEW YORK

*The pilot telling the story of Hudson.*

(See page 59.)

# THE PILOT
# OF THE MAYFLOWER

## A Tale of the Children
## of the Pilgrim Republic

BY

HEZEKIAH BUTTERWORTH

AUTHOR OF TRUE TO HIS HOME, THE WAMPUM BELT, ETC.

*ILLUSTRATED*

NEW YORK AND LONDON
## D. APPLETON AND COMPANY
1916
4325

Sword, pot, and platter of Miles Standish.

# PREFACE.

THIS volume, the eighth of the Creators of Liberty Series, although it should really have been the first, is for the most part but fact in picture. The voyage of the May-flower is one of the most important events in the history of the New World, and the writer has sought to bring into his narrative all the known incidents that took place on the ship during this voyage, which brought our own Argonauts to our shores. While the methods of fiction have been employed in the story, they have not departed from the his-torical spirit. As a method of fiction, the good pilot of the Mayflower has been made a story-teller, but his stories are substantially true. The incident of the jackscrew and the service that it rendered, and that of the copper chain, so far as such a chain became a gift from the Pilgrims to Massa-soit, and was made by that chief a sign of peace in his rela-tions to the colony, were suggested by the Pilgrims' own records. The decision of all the Pilgrims who survived the great sickness not to return with the Mayflower, but to struggle on for the cause of human liberty, is one of the noblest examples of moral heroism, and the first Thanksgiving in the colony, with Massasoit for a guest, closes in a picturesque way the narrative of the decisive part of a history which will ever be sacred to America and the English race. These events it has been our aim to present in pen picture.

The other volumes of this series of books have been successful in finding a large audience of young readers, for which the writer is grateful. The story of the children of the Mayflower is a haunting theme. He has sought to make this interpretation of the life of the young Pilgrims of the Mayflower the best of the series, and he will be glad if it should awaken an interest to study the Pilgrims' literature in those original documents that are now placed within the reach of all.

It was a Greek adage that " A people are known by the heroes they crown." It is true of our own land. The Pilgrim Fathers followed the faith of Columbus in moral enterprise. They stood firm in the storms that would have wrecked common lives, and have added their names to those who walked by faith in the great and decisive events of human history.

H. B.

28 Worcester Street, Boston, Mass.

# CONTENTS.

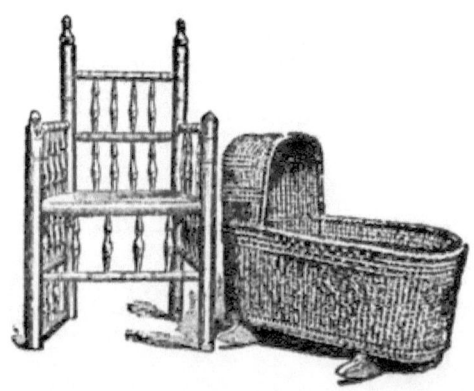

Elder Brewster's chair and cradle of Peregrine White, Pilgrim Hall.

Governor Carver's chair and ancient spinning-wheel, Pilgrim Hall.

# LIST OF ILLUSTRATIONS.

Pilgrim Hall, Plymouth.

# THE PILOT OF THE MAYFLOWER.

## CHAPTER I.

### THE PILOT AND THE INDIANS.

"Beautiful Leyden!"

It was a rugged Scottish sailor who spoke. He had been a fisherman on the coasts of New England and the Banks of Newfoundland. He was among the few sailors that had ever seen these mysterious coasts, for the time was the spring of 1620. He was held to be a wonderful man in those remarkable times, for he had seen American Indians.

A man who had seen American Indians before 1620 never wanted companionship. These Indians were to the Europeans the children of Nature, about whom every one

1

wished to hear.   Columbus had awakened a strange and
vivid curiosity in the dusky race, as he had presented to
Isabella the bejeweled Caribs, with splendid figures and
strong arms holding aloft gorgeous birds, on the occasion of
the festival at Santa Fé in honor of the discovery of the
New World.   Captain John Smith had thrilled England
with Indian tales, to which was added the sylvan romance
of Pocahontas, who had died at Gravesend in 1617, a convert to the Christian faith and the wife of a gallant Englishman.

These were times before De Foe and his nursery-haunt-
ing narrative of Robinson Crusoe, but all men who had seen
Indians were like De Foes in the public eye.

Delightful as were such sea adventurers, traders, and
fishermen to men and women, they were as giants in the
imagination of the children.   What child had not heard of
the lovely Pocahontas, of how she stayed the war club, and
of her marriage amid the English hedgerows?

Sebastian Cabot, in 1502, had brought three Indians
from Newfoundland to England, and had presented them
to Henry VII.   They were the first Indians ever seen in
England.   What were their names?   We do not know.
What became of them?   We do not know, but this we are
pleased to know, that they filled England with wonder.
We are told that when they were found in America they
were clothed with skins of beasts and lived on raw flesh,
"but that, after two years' residence in England, they were

seen in the king's court clothed like Englishmen." And this was in those far, wise days of Henry VII, nearly one hundred years before the Pilgrim Fathers began their wanderings.

In 1576 Captain Martin Frobisher brought to England an Indian whose history was more strange than romantic. He had attracted him to his ship by the ringing of a bell, and so seized him, canoe and all. The savage retained his native fierceness, and we are told that he inflicted terrible injuries upon himself, not being able to injure others. He died of England's cold. There were hearts that pitied him, both for his sufferings and for the injustice that had been done him.

The Scottish sailor whom we introduced to the reader with the words " Beautiful Leyden " was approaching the quaint Holland city on a very remarkable undertaking. He was to pilot the Pilgrim Fathers, or the younger part of the exiled church of John Robinson, from Leyden to Southampton, and thence to the New World, where he had been before, and had seen Indians.

His name was Robert Coppin, a hardy, simple, truehearted Scotchman, and his services had been secured in England by one Thomas Nash, who was bringing him to Leyden to meet the Pilgrims, then preparing to cross the sea.

"Our pilot," they came to call him, and there is such tenderness and significance in the words that we must use him for the character by which to interpret the life of the

children of the Pilgrims on board the Speedwell, the Mayflower, on the smooth, pleasant waters of the early part of
the voyage that changed the history of mankind, on the billows of the storms that followed, and then among the Indians on the rude and wintry New England coast. "Our
pilot" has a friendly sound, and this pilot had a kindly
heart.

Robert Coppin, "our pilot," might well exclaim "Beautiful Leyden!" He had seen many cities in his day, but
never one like this on the borders of the old Rhine. Leyden
was the oldest city in Holland; here were the ruins of a for-
tress founded before Christ; here was a city of heroes.

When it had been besieged by the Spaniards, the Prince
of Orange had broken the dikes and let in the sea.

Then the prince said to the people:

"As a compensation for your losses I will remit your
taxes or build you a university. Which shall it be?"

The people chose the university. It stood there now,
with its roofs glimmering over the canals and above the
lime trees.

The people had chosen well; some of the greatest schol-
ars of Europe are associated with the University of Leyden.

Robert Coppin, the pilot, who had seen Indians, drifted
up one of the canals under the lime trees. The spring was
waning; the trees were filled with song birds and the gardens
with flowers.

"Thomas Nash," said the merry sailor, "why do the

Separatists wish to leave this goodly place? Why do they not remain here?"

He saw the church, the tiled roofs, the pleasant gables and open lattices, and the long lines of water streets or canals.

"There are not many towns like this," he added. "One could stay here forever, if his soul were only content."

"But the souls of these people are not content."

"Why, why, Thomas Nash? Have they not liberty?" asked our pilot.

Some children came down to the landing under the lime trees. Among them was Ellen More, who had found a home in the family of Edward Winslow, and who was to become a little Pilgrim on the Mayflower by and by.

"Yes," said Thomas Nash, "they have liberty, but they fear that it will not last. Yonder is the common cause of the discontent."

"What—the children?"

"Yes, the children. The Separatists wish to found a home where their children can enjoy religious freedom and be educated. Go with me to their meetings and you shall hear."

They landed under the lime trees.

The Scottish seaman felt a little touch on his hand.

He looked down into a child's face. It was a beautiful face, amid waving hair.

"What is your name, my girl?"

" Ellen More."

" Do you belong to the Brownites?"  The Brownites were a sect of dissenters.

" Elizabeth Winslow keeps me, sir.  She is not my own mother, but she is a good, good mother to me.  May I ask you something, sir? "

" Aye, aye—ask on; prattle like yours always holds me. What is it you would know? "

" Are you a pilot, sir? "

" Aye, aye."

" Are you to be our pilot, sir? "

" Aye, aye; and I'll pilot true such girls as you, and I would die for such a crew.  You see I can talk in rhymes."

" And mother Elizabeth said that you had seen Indians. Will you tell us children all about what you saw in New England some day, sir? "

" Aye, aye, my pet; some day—my heart hugs you to think of it—some day, some day, when I am off duty upon the open sea.  I have heard of your foster father before," he added.  " Edward Winslow; he has been a great traveler.  He is rich, and he is much esteemed, and he is going to leave this beautiful city, and all, and take you with him, my pet.  Oh, this is a beautiful world; and God is good, I'm thinking, but men's hearts are hard.  I will tell you about the Indian that I saw some day."

" And you will tell all the children, sir? "

"Yes, yes, you great little heart, all. How many will there be of you?"

"Twelve little ones, and as many young folks, I heard mother Elizabeth say."

"That is quite a company of children and young people."

"But you are to be our pilot."

"I must go now—methinks such as you ought to have a better pilot than I. And you have, though I am a rough man that says it—you have, you have. Such as you have a Pilot that the eye does not see."

He left the canoe and followed Thomas Nash to the house of John Robinson, the pastor of the church in Leyden. The place where the goodly man's house stood is still marked in Leyden. It is near the great church, which is also inscribed, the tablets being the gifts of grateful sons of the Pilgrims in America.

Then Robert Coppin, our pilot, stood face to face with this aged man, the prophet of America, who was to build beyond the seas, but never to go to the new colony that he had builded.

There was to be a gathering of the exiles in that house that day. The pilot would hear what these people had to say, and then he would better understand their case and cause. Perhaps he would meet there again the sweet face of Ellen More, if the Winslows should come to the meeting. He hoped he would, for he was a lonely man, and the child's touch had made him very happy.

2

There are people that it is a blessing for a lonely heart to know, and little Ellen More, to whom Edward Winslow had given a home, was one of them.

The little girl came to the meeting as the pilot had hoped. She was led by the hand of a lovely lady, Mistress Elizabeth Winslow.

After the religious exercises were over, Pastor John Robinson said: " Our pilot is here, a lusty Scotchman whom we are glad to welcome. He brings to us a letter from Robert Cushman, our English agent. This letter I will read."

He read the letter, which stated that the Mayflower, a ship of one hundred and eighty tons, Thomas Jones master, would soon leave London for Southampton, and take there a company of English immigrants, who would sail in her to the Hudson River.

The Mayflower! It was probably the first time that John Robinson's people heard the name! It was to be a ship of destiny, the winged messenger of heaven to the western world!

The people listened to the tidings with intense interest.

" But," said John Robinson, " this is not the most important information to us now and here that our good Scotch pilot has brought. The letter further says that a sixty-ton pinnace, the Speedwell, has been purchased by the Adventurers, our company, and that she is to be fitted out here in Holland, and that she is to take you to Southampton, and to go with the Mayflower to the new country, and is to remain there for a year. I will read you this part of the letter."

There was silence as he read this part of the letter which so concerned the pastor's congregation. He then said pleasantly: "Our pilot here has seen the New World, and he may be able to tell us what we need most to carry. Speak out, Robert Coppin, our people have eager ears to hear you!"

Robert Coppin, "our pilot," holding his hat in his hand, bowed low and said:

"May it please your reverence and your honors, if I may thus address you, who do not desire titles or any flattering words, the best things that you can carry, which you do not now have, are, in my humble opinion, presents for the Indian chiefs."

"That is a good thought," said Edward Winslow, who had traveled much, and had read the letter of Sir Walter Raleigh and other adventurers in the New World. "A very good thought, Master Coppin; and may I ask what trifles most please the Indians on these new coasts?"

"Chains for the neck," said he, "and belts for the waist. The Indians wear chains made of shells. Free chains among these people are emblems of dignity and power. A chain that holds a treasure that can lie upon the breast is very highly esteemed by the lords of the forest."

"But," said Mr. Winslow, "we would hardly be able to carry to them gold or silver chains."

"A copper chain with a medal would do as well," said

the pilot. "You can buy such chains at the shops in the town."

Little Ellen More's eyes danced. "A copper chain with a medal for a chief," said she to her foster mother, Elizabeth Winslow, when the two had gone out upon the street. "I wish that I had such a chain."

Our pilot had joined Mistress Elizabeth Winslow and Ellen, and had heard what Ellen had said.

"I will buy you a copper chain and medal if your mother is willing, little girl," said he.

"May I carry it over the sea?"

"If the mistress wills."

"And give it to an Indian chief?"

"If she so wills." The answer made light the steps of the girl.

They came to a shop where jewels, rings, and chains with medals of Holland were sold, and our pilot asked them to enter the place. He there purchased a copper chain with a medal, and put it over Ellen's neck.

"See," said he, "it reaches nearly to the floor. "But an Indian is tall and big."

"You are very kind to my little girl," said Elizabeth Winslow. "I am glad indeed that we are to have you for our pilot. I love them that love children; such people are true friends to all men, and I can read your heart."

The pilot wondered if indeed the copper chain would ever find an Indian chief.

# CHAPTER II.

In the houses in the neighborhood many of the people were preparing their goods or effects for removal to the quay where lay the ship that was to take them to Southampton and thence across the sea, three thousand miles wide, to a wilderness as wide as the sea.

The immigrants had sold most of their household property, but each had retained something that he wished to take to the new land. This one had a chair that he wished to keep; that one a stand or table with sacred associations. Elder Brewster had a chest and a looking-glass. The chest is still to be seen in Pilgrim Hall, Plymouth; America's "Ark of the Covenant" it came to be, on account of the purpose to which it was put on the last days of the voyage of the Mayflower. Of this we will tell you the story in its place. The looking-glass which, with Elder Brewster's Bible, may still be seen at Plymton, near Plymouth, in an ancient Brewster house, is perhaps the most precious of all American mirrors. Into it all of the Pilgrim fathers and mothers may have looked, including Robinson of Leyden, their old pastor, who expected to follow them when the

11

younger members of the church should have planted their
church in the wilderness, but who was called to make another
pilgrimage from which none return.

Every one seemed to wish to take on board the little ship
more articles than it could be allowed to carry.

As soon as it became known that the pilot had come and
was at the house of the Pilgrim pastor, the boys and young
men began to gather there to meet him.  They wished to
see a man who had been to the land whither they were going.
Among the boys was Jasper More, a brother of little Ellen
More, of the Winslow family.  Love Brewster and Wrastle
Brewster, sons of the amiable Elder Brewster, as also John
Billington and John Hooke, a servant in the Allerton
family.

At last the day before that set for the departure came.
The children gathered with the others at Robinson's house.

They were a merry group on this serious day.  John
Robinson seems to have loved young people, and to have won
them as a common father.  They appealed to him when in
doubt, and he decided their cases with a sympathetic heart.
A friend of mankind is always the children's friend.

Two of the boys and a carpenter came bringing a jackscrew.  They wished to take it on board the ship.  The
boys were carrying the screw, and the carpenter was following them.

"That is a curious instrument that you have there, my
friend," said Elder Robinson to the carpenter.  "It is not

great for size, but they tell me that there is power in it,"
looking toward the pilot.

"Aye, aye, sir, that there is. There has been many a
ship saved from wreckage by a jackscrew. Are you going
to take it on board?"

"That is what I would do," said the carpenter. "But
they say that we are in danger of overloading the ship with
storage, that nothing more must go on board of the barges
which are to take us to the ship—not so much as an axe or
hatchet. That instrument might prove very much of service in case of a strain on the ship during the voyage."

"Which may Heaven prevent," said good Elder Robinson. "It is the duty of people to live where they can do the
most good, and carry with them where they go the things
that will be most useful. I am not the captain of the ship,
but if I were I would admit the jackscrew."

"But, my good man," said Coppin, "may it please you,
I am to be the pilot and so one of the mates, and I know the
value of a jackscrew. We may see hard weather before we
reach the American coast. I will take it on board; the
captain will not object to that. It is small baggage that I
will have to carry."

One of the boys shouted—"Our pilot!"

"Aye, aye, boys; it is good hearts that ye have to say
that. Put down the jackscrew under the trees, until after
the meeting has been held, and I will see that it is taken
on board the ship from the barges. I am to be pilot of

this goodly company, thank Heaven, and to do your bidding."

"Our pilot!" said the boys. They all felt that there was something in the Scotchman's heart to trust.

"I am glad, my boys, of all this good will. I have seen the shores on which you are going to settle. I am going with you, and my heart as well as my hand shall be true to you. I wish that I were going to share your lot, but that will never be the fate of Robert Coppin, the sailor and fisherman; he must follow the sea, he must follow the sea!"

"You have seen the Indians," said Jasper More.

"Aye, aye; I have seen a forest king in all of his wampum and feathers, with his bow and quiver, and his lusty men."

"Will they harm us where we settle?" asked Love Brewster.

"No, no, I mind not, or they would not have done so if the captains on the coast had not stolen some of them and carried them away."

"Will you tell us about those stolen Indians?" asked Wrastle Brewster.

"Aye, aye, my lads, some day, some pleasant day on the sea. The people are gathering now, and Elder Brewster desires me to stay to this godly meeting."

"Yes, yes, my good sailor," said the elder, "I wish you to stay that you may see what a precious freight you are to pilot to the unknown shore. Men's hearts are more than any gold that they can possess, and it is the worth that is invisible that determines the destinies of men. It is the elect of time that you are to meet to-day, sir, and to pilot into the empty world where Heaven has opened the gate of opportunity. I like you well, sir, I like you well. But no more now; the people are coming, and this is our last day together here! "

Robert Coppin bowed his head.

The boys took off their hats and shouted again: " Our pilot! "

The Scotchman watched the people as they gathered. How noble and yet how simple they looked! Captain Carver and his wife; William Brewster, the deacon, and Mistress Brewster; Edward Winslow and Mistress Winslow, and beautiful little Ellen More; William Bradford and Mistress Bradford; Isaac Allerton and his family; Captain Miles Standish and Rose Standish; William Mullins, his wife, and the afterward historic Priscilla, then a Puritan girl; the Hopkinsons; the Billingtons; the Tilleys; the Chiltons; and John Alden, who was one day to marry Priscilla. Many were young people. Their dress was simple; they wore the crown of character. They had dwelt together in Leyden in love and unity for nearly twelve years—pilgrims, led by an invisible hand.

He watched them there as they came toward the house through the sunny streets cooled by the lime trees. It was a silent throng—as still as the placid canals. Some of the women were weeping.

He saw the children as they came. Pastor Robinson was to speak especially of the children and to them that day. Ellen More and her brother Jasper had already interested him, and his heart went out in pitying love to them because they were dependent on others, and in a sense alone in the world. He could feel for broken families and be as arms, heart, and guidance to such, for such was his nature.

The sun rose high over the canals and the lime trees. The storks sat listlessly on the chimneys and gables. The black flat-bottomed boats lay idling on the waters. In the square students in dark habits passed thoughtfully to and fro. Leyden is beautiful now; it was so in 1620.

Why were these people going out of these serene streets on the Rhine across an uncertain sea into a wilderness of savages, wild beasts, and tangled trees? Why? why? the pilot asked as he stood there and wondered.

There was not a church, a school, a roof in all the land to which they were going. Not a single road. The blazed trail of the red hunter was there; the frail tent of bark and skins. Not a library was there on all the shining shores. The forest lords knew not their own history. They were probably the descendants of some wandering Asiatic race. Their gods were the beings of a rude imagination. They had not the vices of the old nations, but to shed blood was their glory, and revenge was the sweetest passion of life. The race that seeks blood will perish.

Why? why?

The people had assembled now in the great room. He would go in and stand by the door, holding his hat in his hand. He would hear what the grave and gentle pastor had to say. This was to be the good man's last discourse. He would listen intently. The pastor should answer the questions that kept rising in his mind on this late midsummer day, amid the beautiful serenity that ends in the low Rhine lands the last shortening days of July.

What will the pastor say? He will at least tell his people, his young people, why he wills them to go.

The young people all bent a friendly look on the pilot as they passed into the room. The children sat so that they could look upon him, as he stood there with his bowed head, hat in hand. He had seen many strange seas—the Spanish Main, the island of Newfoundland. They had been told this; and he had seen a red Indian king.

# CHAPTER III.

THE room was still. The occasional sob of a woman caused the children's faces to wear a look of sympathy and wonder. One woman spoke aloud to another who was deaf, breaking the silence. She said, "Not one of us will ever see this place again, not one!"

John Robinson arose, bowed his head in silence, and then read Luther's version of Psalm C, which the company sung.

The house had very large rooms, and a garden which was a kind of park and now blowing with flowers. In Robinson's garden were some twenty or more cabins, and here the poor people lived. His congregation worshiped in his house, and the place where this socialistic community dwelt in wonderful harmony and love is now marked with the beautiful inscription:

"ON THIS SPOT LIVED, TAUGHT, AND DIED,
JOHN ROBINSON, 1611–1625."

Robinson's congregation must have numbered some five hundred. The Dutch came to love this wandering church, and gathered about the doors of the church, home, and garden.

18

Such people were gathering now, and a whisper went round that it was the pilot who was standing hat in hand in the door.

"It is sorry that we are that they are going," said a rugged Hollander to the pilot in English. "It is kind hearts that they have, and there is never one of them but pays his debts. They all know the meaning of the text, 'Owe no man anything'; ah, they do speak the truth and pay their debts, but they dispute about doctrines, much is the pity, I think. What have you here outside?"

The pilot looked down on the blooming grass, and saw it was the jackscrew to which the Hollander alluded.

"It is a tool that I am going to put on board the boats that go to the ship as soon as the meeting is over," said the pilot.

Here the pastor arose again and spread out his hands. How holy and noble he looked! There were tears in his eyes, but his face glowed.

"Here," said the Hollander to the pilot, "take it away."

"What, my friend?" asked the pilot.

"That jackscrew; it is out of harmony with the place; this is a spot where one should take off his shoes, I mind; and that thing looks like a trespasser—a sinner, it is a worldly thing—let me take it out into the garden."

"Your spiritual sense is keen indeed, my friend," said the pilot.

The old Dutchman took the jackscrew and carried it into

the garden and set it down amid the flowers, then took it up again and left it among some weeds, "where it belonged," as he said as he came back and looked into the door again.

John Robinson prayed. The prayer seemed to rise into the regions of spiritual mystery, and the reverent old Hollander listened as though a very prophet was speaking.

Then the pastor uttered the strange words "By the River Ahava."

The pilot listened.

What did it mean? He had never heard of that river before; in all of his sailings and wanderings he had not found it.

Then Robinson repeated an ancient record from sacred Hebrew history:

"And there at the river by Ahava, I proclaimed a fast, that we might humble ourselves before God, and seek a right way for us, and for our children, and all our substance."

He related the Hebrew story that had left this simple record. He preached from each clause, but when he came to speak on the clause "and for our children" the room was silent, and the pilot stepped within the door. Robert Coppin saw that the pastor had made in his interpretation the Zuyder Zee a River Ahava, and that "our children" were a cause of the event of this memorable day.

"Why do you venture upon the ocean," said Robinson in substance, "to find a home in an unknown land? This is a pleasant place, amid the lime trees, the canals, the sea

meadows, the ancient homes, and the towers of learning and
the spires of faith? Why do you leave the pleasant lands of
the vineyards of the Rhine? Children, hear me; ye young
people whom I have so much loved, and shall always love,
listen to me; 'tis the last time that I shall open to you my
heart.

" It is for your sakes that the boats that are to bear you to
the Speedwell will sail in the cool of the day.

" It is England that has caused you to go into exile, but
her blood flows in our veins; we love her history, her name,
and we must remain Englishmen. In Holland, by the pleasant sea, you are losing your language. This must not be.
The language of old England, of the heroes of faith, of the
homes of our fathers, must be kept sacred. It will be so in
the wilderness.

" You are changing in character here. The habits of a
city of luxury are taking away your strength of soul. Your
faith must be kept pure; wealth is nothing, fame is nothing,
character is all.

" You must be educated; all of you must be educated
in the free air of faith. There must be planted for you in
the wilderness a place where education shall be free.

" My children, I may never be able to follow you into the
wilderness. It matters not. Your parents may suffer—it
matters not, if so be it is Heaven's will. It matters not if you
can be educated for a higher life of the freedom of the faith
that the suffering world waits.

"Go forth, go forth, prisoners of hope. All light has not yet been revealed. New light will break forth from the world in the wilderness. Some minds can go as far as Luther, some as far as Calvin, some can see truth in very vision, but do you not resist new truth, and you must only follow me as far as I follow the truth of Christ!"

The pilot saw, as it were, the serene pastor's soul. The purpose of the pilgrims was now clear to him. They were to face the perils of the world, of the seas, and the wilderness, not for themselves, but for their children; not for their own comfort, but for the comfort of those who were to come after them. They loved welfare more than wealth, and others more than themselves.

Many of them had become poor for this purpose of the help of mankind. They were not going to seek for riches, they were leaving worldly riches behind. They had turned their backs on ease and comfort and the hopes of peace, all of which might have been theirs.

When and where in all history was there ever an assembly like this?

At the close of the discourse, the communion was administered to those who were to go and those who were to stay. That scene is worthy of a painting.

Then they went out into the great garden, many of them leading the children by the hand.

The pilot went out to find his jackscrew in the weeds "where it belonged." He took it up, and was about to make his way with it toward the barges that were to go down the canals to the Speedwell, when he was met by a sea captain who had come up here from Delftshaven.

"They will all wish to come back again," said the captain, in the hearing of the company.

"Pilot," said Elder Brewster, "you have been to the country; do you think that we shall ever wish to come back again?"

"Nay, nay," said the pilot, "a man's country is in his soul. Nay, nay, not one of you will ever wish to come back."

But the captain's words echoed.

"Shall we wish to return with you again, when the ship lifts her wings for old England, I wonder?" said Elizabeth Winslow. "O pilot, those words of the captain's are a hawk in the sky. What do you think?"

"Shall we wish to come back?" said Rose Standish, echoing the dark prophecy.

"Nay, nay," said the pilot. "Come back? Did you ever hear a woman wish to return from any place where were the best prospects for her children? Come back, come back? No; it is prospects that make the heart happy. Present hardship is nothing if the future is bright."

"But the Israelites longed for the fleshpots of Egypt," said one who had heard what the captain had said.

"There are no Israelites of that kind here, please your honor," said the pilot. "The world grows better, else what is the use of the world?"

3

"Right, right you are," said Parson Robinson. "There will never be an age when there will be not a better one to come. The world will be better when we go out of it than when we came into it, or it ought to be. Whatever happens to this one or that, it matters not; it is the destiny of these people to sail. God's time has come. The sea may rage, the savages of an unknown land may uplift their weapons of war, but the time has come for the truth to make a new nation of free men, who may own their souls, and found a new nation in faith."

The pilot turned away and went down to the boats that were to take them to the Speedwell which lay at Delftshaven, some ten or more miles away.

Little Ellen More ran after him.

"O pilot, pilot, do you think that we will ever want to come back again?"

"No, no, my little one, you will never come back again," said the pilot.

His words were prophetic. Little Ellen More would never come back.

Of their departure on that day of the glowing prophecy of Robinson, and of the dark words of Captain Bradford, the leader wrote a single sentence that might well be set in gold. Were we to be asked what is the most beautiful sentence in all history, we would say it was this:

"So they left that goodly and pleasant city which had been their resting place near twelve years, but they knew

*The embarkation of the Pilgrims.*

that they were pilgrims, and looked not much on those things, but lifted up their eyes to the heavens, their dearest country, and quieted their spirits."

The words pictured Robinson's own soul, which was the sentiment of all.

That evening the company went on board the boats that were to convey them to the Speedwell at Delftshaven; they started for the ship early in the morning, and Robinson went with them.

Some of the children wished to go in the boat with the pilot, and they were allowed so to do. The older colonists sought the boat of Robinson, Brewster, and Carver, that they might talk with him as they went along the canal in the late midsummer day.

The barges were moored near the Nan's Bridge, opposite the Klok-steeg, where Robinson's house and garden were.

They were to go by the way of the Vliet, as a part of the canal between Leyden and Delft was called. They would pass a water gate. After some nine miles on the Vliet they would come to a city and wide canal called The Hague. They would here find the still placid waters lined with noble trees, and they would pass in view of Oud-Delft, and the Old Kirk with its lancet windows, and perhaps in sight of the red-tiled house in which William the Silent, the father of the cause of liberty in the Netherlands, had thirty-six years before been assassinated. They would pass the gates of Delft,

and leave the town, and enter the Delftshaven Canal, at the
end of which their ship would appear.

The dikes were high in this part of the Low Countries,
and the tide was full, and they found themselves sailing
above the land. They may have stopped at Delft, and
probably did. If so, their journey lasted a large part of
the day.

And now they are upon the canals.

As they passed the gates of Delft, and beheld the slender
spire fading against the sky, Elizabeth Winslow called the
children around her, and pointed out to them the red gables
of the palace of William the Silent.

"Who was William the Silent?" asked litle Ellen More
of her foster mother.

"He was the defender of the liberties of the people of
Holland. Had he not been, it is probable that we should
never have found in that colony a home. For the sake of
liberty he broke the dikes of the sand dunes and let in the
sea. And the sea fought for Holland. He died a martyr,
and his last thoughts were for liberty."

They were approaching the village of Overschie, and the
children asked Mistress Elizabeth to tell them the story of
the death of William in the cause of liberty, because of this
tragedy all the people had heard.

Mistress Elizabeth was not loth to speak of these things
with the fading town of Delft, that she would never see
more, still in view.

### THE STORY OF THE SILENT PRINCE.

"William," she said, taking Ellen More in her arms, "was a man of few words and wonderful wisdom in council. So they called him William the Taciturn, or William the Silent. He was bred to courts, and he lived in a very splendid way; but when he espoused the cause of liberty he sold his valuables and gave up all show and vainglory, and was glad to live like one of the people. He announced himself a convert to the Holland faith, and asked to lead the armies of the Netherlands in the cause of liberty.

"His love for the cause of the liberty of the people grew, until he thought and dreamed of nothing else. He felt that Heaven had given this cause to him, and that he was invisibly, as it were, in the little country of the dikes leading the hopes of mankind.

"The war for liberty was waged against Philip of Spain, who claimed the country for the Spanish crown.

"William was sometimes successful and sometimes defeated in a long war, but in 1579 he laid the foundation of the Dutch Republic, and Holland and Zeeland proclaimed him their Stadtholder.

"But Philip of Spain, enraged at the loss of the country which he claimed as his hereditary right, offered twenty-five thousand gold crowns for his head.

"Perilous days were his then. He went about his new republic of freedom as a marked man. The town of Delft was beset with mysterious men—ruffians, some of them, perhaps, Spaniards in disguise, some Italians, all adventurers, whose presence was suspected and feared.

"There was a little, thin, dark-minded man named Balthazar Gerard, who appeared before the Prince of Parma, in the interest of the Spanish king, and asked for money to go to Delft as a pretended refugee. The money was refused, but a councilor of the prince said to him: 'Go forth and defray your own expenses, and if you succeed the king will reward you, and you shall make yourself an immortal name.'

"He came to Delft pretending to be a friend to William. He obtained a commission to go to France, and there was made a commissioner to bear dispatches to the Dutch court, and was admitted into the presence of the prince.

"When he met the prince with the dispatches he trembled. He had come unarmed this time, and he had prepared for no way of escape; but the prince's door was open to him now, and he would come again.

"On Sunday morning, as the bells were tolling, Balthazar entered the courtyard.

"'What brings you here to-day?' asked the sergeant of the halberdiers.

"'I would like to go to church across the way,' said the wily conspirator, 'but see, I have only this travel-stained attire, without fit shoes or hose.'

"The little dusty stranger with his pious words did not

excite the suspicion of the guard. The latter spoke to an officer about the matter, and the officer probably asked the prince for money that the messenger of France might be able to appear at church decently.

"William's heart responded to the appeal, and he furnished Balthazar with the money for his own ruin.

"On Tuesday, July 10, 1584, the dinner hour was announced in the palace. The prince with his wife on his arm, followed by the ladies and gentlemen of his family, started to enter the dining room. The prince was dressed like a plain man. He wore a beggar's hat, a high ruff, and a loose surcoat of gray.

"As he passed along the white face of a little man met him in the doorway.

"'I have come for my passport, prince,' said the little man.

"'Who is that?—what does he mean?' asked the princess, noticing with alarm the pallor of the man's face.

"'Merely a person who has come for a passport,' said he. 'Give him one,' he said to his secretary.

"'I never saw so villainous a face,' said the princess to William in an undertone.

"The company passed on to the tables. After the meal William came out into the vestibule, and began to ascend the stairway, upon the left side of which was a recess. Suddenly there was a report of a pistol, and the prince fell back, exclaiming:

"'O my God, have mercy upon my soul! O my God, have mercy upon my poor people!'

"His sister rushed toward him, and saw that he was dying.

"'Do you commend your soul to Christ?' she asked.

"'I do,' he answered, and soon after expired in the arms of his wife.

"Balthazar had accomplished his purpose. He was captured and torn to pieces. This is a terrible tale for you to hear, but if we should ever lay the foundation of a free colony, and it should grow, we shall owe much to him who perished for liberty under the red roofs of yonder palace."

The children looked back. It was, as we may suppose, near night now. Delft was fading.

The placid canal that led to the port was near. They still had some miles to go. We can not be sure of the time, but we will suppose it to be near nightfall when the barges drifted into the last canal.

"That is a hard story, little Ellen More," said our pilot, "but you should know what liberty costs."

"The Indians could not do a more terrible thing than that," said she. And she added: "The great chief will be good to us, for we will give him the copper chain."

# CHAPTER IV.

In the long summer twilight and evening the Pilgrims
drifted along the still waters of the canal between Delft and
Delftshaven, which is now as it was then. The water runs
on a level with the wide green plain, on which flocks and
herds grazed then as now. The great fans of windmills
turned in the air. Around the mills were farm sheds, with
walks of powdered shells, and flower gardens that were fan-
tastically arranged amid the green lawns and that blazed
with color. As they passed the gates of Delft, two airy
fortalices shadowed the warm, flower-scented air. They
could not sleep. Winslow says that " the night was passed
with little sleep for the most, but with friendly entertainment
and Christian discourse." There must have been several
boats, for the Pilgrims numbered one hundred and two, and
the people who went to Delftshaven to bid them a last farewell in the morning were many, and their baggage was great,
for many of the exiles had been or were people of means.

The way from the fortalices of Delft to Delftshaven
was a clear one. We will picture it as taking place late in

31

the day. The weather was mild. The pilot had little to do, and the children turned from Mistress Elizabeth Winslow to him, and when he sat down after the afterglow had faded, Ellen More said:

"You said that you would tell us of the Indians that you have met in your voyages."

"Aye, aye, that I did, my little Pilgrim, and if it suits you well I will tell you of one that I have seen. He was a chief, or a sagamore, or lord, but I did not find him on the coast of the new land at all; I met him in England."

The children and young people gathered closely around the pilot.

"Ah! ah! what are you about to do?" said Captain Reynolds. "Away with your story-telling, but I would not refuse to hear something entertaining myself now, seeing everything is so quiet; there is a bit of the child left in me yet, and I will take a seat among the children and be a child in my ears, as I used to be when my father told sea tales of the Hebrides. Go on, go on, and I'll not bother you. The ship goes fair."

### THE STRANGE STORY OF TUSQUANTO.

"There is a country on the cool side of the sea which Sir Francis Drake first saw, which some call New Albion, but which he named New England. There is a harbor there which the Virginia Company call Plymouth, from our Plymouth. It is a fine country in summer time; great vines are there, heavy with grapes; the sea is full of fish, and the sky of birds; but oh, the winters—o-o-o-oh! may you never see the like, or hear the wind blow there!

"Who has not heard of Sir Ferdinando Gorges? He was the friend of Raleigh, you know, and the enemy of Essex, as all Englishmen have heard, and he served Elizabeth with so much valor on the sea that the crown made him Governor of Plymouth in 1604—the Plymouth of the oaks, the grapes, the harbors of fish, where the sky is full of wings, and the summers are so lovely, and the wind blows so cold.

"Now Plymouth is called by the Indians Pawtuxet, and some fifteen or sixteen years ago Captain Weymouth, one of the knight's captains, found at this town of Pawtuxet a solitary Indian, a lord, a sagamore, or chief, who told a terrible tale. Listen to it—it haunts me sometimes when I am all alone.

"The Indian said that all of his people were dead. That a great blight had fallen upon them; that they suddenly turned yellow and died, and that there was none left to bury them, and that he alone was left.

"Alone, all alone, he had gone to his tent, and cried out when there was none to hear. He could only say 'alone, alone, alone,' to the sea and the stars.

"Was his story true?

"The sailors went on shore; they entered the evergreen forests, and wandered among the oaks, the vines and rocks, and they found it even as Tusquanto, or Tusquantum, the lonely forest lord, had said.

" 'The people died in heaps,' said the solitary Indian.

" They found that it had been so. There were whole villages of the dead; the bodies lay unburied, with only the ravens to lament for them.

" So Tusquanto was left alone with the dead nation, crying out on the shores that blossomed still, though the people were dead.

" Captain Weymouth told the wandering chief of his own land, of England over the sea. He told him, I think, of his master Sir Ferdinando, who would welcome such as he. I hope this is so, for some think that he carried Tusquanto away as captive; but be this as it may, Captain Weymouth sailed away from Plymouth with Tusquanto, the only surviving Indian of Pawtuxet. Now if I were a poet I would write a poem about Tusquanto and his lament for the dead tribes.

" Sir Ferdinando, of the Virginia Colonization Company, was delighted to meet the Indian lord. He took him to his courtly home, and instructed him in the English language. He taught him how to talk, that the Indian might tell him about the country and people over the sea.

" Marvelous were the tales that the Indian began to tell. Sir Ferdinando used to say that the more he conversed with him the better hope he gave him of the lands over which he had been made governor. Tusquanto told him of goodly rivers in the new country, of mountains that pierced the sky, of roaring waterfalls, of harbors rich in fish, of fruits that delighted the taste.

"He kept Tusquanto for three years, and then loaded him with gifts and sent him back to New England as a land pilot with Captain Thomas Dermer, a sea rover in his service.

"Dermer went to the land of the dead a year ago to see if the tales that Tusquanto had told Sir Ferdinando were true.

"The men from the ship, guided by Tusquanto, entered the forests. The woods were still, save the birds singing there. Grand trees and great lakes were there. It was a glorious country. Tusquanto had spoken truly.

"They came to a place called Namasket, now Middleboro, Massachusetts.

"Tusquanto had told them of a great forest king named Massasoit. He lived at Pokonoket, a land of green woods and bright rivers, a day's journey away. Captain Dermer sent a message to this great forest king.

"Two kings came to meet him. One of them may have been a brother to the great king. They were clad in glittering shells, in plumes, and were followed by stately men with bows and quivers of arrows.

"Captain Dermer wondered when these giants appeared. He had great reason for surprise, as you shall hear.

"**One of the forest lords approached the captain.**

" 'Your face is white,' cried he. 'You belong to the race that steal. You steal our people from the fishing grounds, and carry them away. You are here to steal, and you shall suffer for your crimes. You shall not return to the ship; follow the chiefs! follow me!'

" 'Captain Dermer is no thief,' pleaded Tusquanto.

" 'The whole pale race are thieves!' cried the red lord. 'They steal our people and carry them away on their great boats with wings. Listen!

" 'Many moons ago we found one of your winged boats off the shore.

" 'We stole up to it at night and burned it, and we carried away three of the men. We have kept them to cut wood and draw water and to make sport for us. They are with us now. You shall follow back the chiefs to cut wood and draw water and make sport for us.

" 'The men that we led captive talk our language now. One of them says that your God will punish us for what we have done to him. But your God can not do it; we are too many—we are too many.' Here the Indian began to dance and cry out, 'We are too many! we are too many!'

"Then Tusquanto said: 'The men whom you hold are innocent. They never meant you harm. You do them wrong to make them captives.'

" 'But your people do the same. You must follow us back, and cut wood and draw water and make sport for us.

Your God can not harm us; we are too many! ' Then he danced again.

" ' I have brought the sea captain here as a messenger of a great king,' said Tusquanto. 'He comes to meet a king as a man of honor. We are not to blame for what others have done. We came to smoke the pipe of peace.'

" Then the great Massasoit spoke.

" ' You are from the king over the sea. We will smoke the pipe of peace together, and I will set the captives that we hold free. Massasoit is a man of honor! '

" Then they smoked the pipe of peace together. It was May time. The birds sang and the Indians danced. There were Indian runners there, and they brought back the white captives after a little time. The captives were Frenchmen.

" Such is my story; it is substantially a true one. I would like to see the great Massasoit. Would not you, my children? "

The young people dreamed over the tale: the silent land; the Indian lord; Tusquanto at the home of Sir Ferdinando; the journey toward the Indian country in the silent woods; and the great king Massasoit, who was governed by a sense of justice, mercy, and honor.

" I wish that we might live in Massasoit's country," said little Ellen More. "It may be that the copper chain is for him. I hope that it is."

So thought all the little Pilgrims.

"We must attend to our own work now, pilot," said Captain Reynolds. "Were I to emigrate, I would go to the country of Massasoit. He must be a godlike chief."

In the last light of the long sunset little Ellen More held up the copper chain. Would that chain ever gleam under the forest trees on the neck of some bronze lord of the far, far West?

# CHAPTER V.

THE rising light of the morning at Delftshaven revealed the outline of the Speedwell, which was to take the Pilgrims to Southampton. The sails of the ship were already set to the fresh breeze. The tide was at its full, and there was given them but a brief time for parting after the baggage was hurried on board. The pastor fell upon his knees and prayed for his flock with streaming eyes.

The full tide beat against the ship and they must be gone. The Union Jack rolled out, and high in the air the pennant blew westward. The ship swung away from the pier and drifted down the channel along the " creeping Maas beyond the isle Ysselmonde. The company fired a volley with small arms, a cannon boomed, the smoke cleared in the sun; Holland faded away, the forms of loved ones vanished; they would never see the country nor their old friends there again. Their sails were set to the west; they were to work the miracle of the ages under the setting sun.

The young folks gathered around the pilot again when they saw that his hands were free. They had dreamed of the Indian chiefs of which he had spoken.

4

He told them another story of an Indian captive who was still alive, and whom perhaps they would sometime meet in the new country, as Indians who could speak English were of great value to the colonists.

### EPENOW, THE INDIAN WONDER.

" It was Sir Ferdinando Gorges who used to tell this tale, and it was a favorite story among the traders who were looking for fortunes beyond the sea.

" ' I was one day surprised,' said Sir Ferdinando, ' to see one Henry Harley come bringing to me an Indian giant.'

" ' " Here is an Indian who can talk English," ' said Harley. ' " He might be valuable to us as a pilot." '

" ' From whence does he come?' asked Sir Ferdinando.

" ' " From near Plymouth. He was captured with twenty-nine other natives, and was taken to Spain to be sold for a slave. He escaped slavery, and was brought to London, and he has been exhibited here as a *wonder*." '

" A wonder he was, lofty in stature, with a haughty face. He used to say ' Welcome! welcome! ' to the crowds who visited him in London. He was a wonder in intellect as well as in body. He acquired the English readily, and he soon set Sir Ferdinando wondering in the most unexpected way, as you shall be told.

" Sir Ferdinando was ambitious, of great wealth, and hoped to hear of a gold mine on the coasts of the northern seas, such as had been found in Peru.

"The Indian wonder came to understand this, and to see in it a way of escape. So one day he began to speak of the golden treasures worn by the Indian lords of Pokonoket and places like that. The eyes of the knight must have enlarged, and his hearing become keen.

"'Gold, Epenow? Did you say gold?'

"'Yes, master, such as your lady wears on her neck. Gold, not wampum, but gold.'

"'Where did your people find this gold?' asked Sir Ferdinando.

"'In the rocks and in the caves.'

"'Do you know where the caves of gold are?' asked the trader.

"'Yes, master. We light our council fires there.'

"'Could you pilot my men to the caves of gold?'

"'Yes, master, yes. The Indian lords mingle gold with their wampum. Gold is as thick as berries in the wampum maker's lodges. I could take your men to the workers in wampum and gold.'

"Sir Ferdinando needed to hear no more. He fitted out a ship and loaded Epenow with presents, and dreamed golden dreams, like the Spanish sailor who went to find the fountain of youth.

"So the tall Epenow became suddenly not only a wonder, but a very great man among the traders, and they sailed away with him, and he feasted the minds of the adventurers with marvelous tales of the treasures of the country.

" He must have told them how many of the people had died of the plague, and they must have imagined that the gathering of treasures would be easy in such a land. This was in June, 1614.

" They came to the Plymouth country, where there were sandy capes and great green islands.

" In the harbor where the ship was moored the wonderful Epenow asked leave to invite his friends on board. They came and he welcomed them lustily, and probably talked much in English for English ears, but he talked with the Indians in the Indian tongue for a very different purpose. Some of these Indians were his relatives, and among them were his brothers.

" You may be sure that he and his brothers met most graciously, and that he had much to say to them that was not in the English tongue.

" When they were gone he said to his English friends:

" ' I have invited my people to come to see me again to-morrow.'

" ' I fear that they would kill thee if it were known to them that thou hadst come to reveal the secrets of their country,' said the captain. ' I must guard thee from harm.'

" Then the captain put upon Epenow flowing garments, so that he could be caught and held, in case his friends should seek to tear him away. He also placed two men over him, to guard him during the visit of his friends.

*The departure from Delftshaven.*

"The next day the Indians came in twenty canoes. How lovely they must have looked in the summer sea!

"Epenow shouted to them in English. What he meant by this I can not say. He and they knew.

"The captain ordered his musketeers to be prepared against any surprise, for all his hopes were centered in the friendly service of the Indian giant, who must have looked very queerly in his flowing robes.

"The Indians drifted about on the sea in their canoes until the captain called to them to come on board. They were armed with bows and arrows.

"The chief men came at the captain's call.

"Epenow was in the hold of the ship. The captain was in the forecastle.

"'Come to me, Epenow,' said the captain.

"Epenow started up and walked toward the captain, the two guards walking beside him.

"Suddenly he was gone. Whence? where? He had vanished. He had stepped back. His loose garments were seen floating in the air, when nothing more was to be found of him. He had gone over the side of the ship.

"'I tried to catch him by his coat,' said a sailor, 'but he could not be stayed.'

"The sailors rushed to the side of the ship, but were met by a flight of arrows.

"The canoes disappeared from the sea as rapidly as Epenow had gone over the side of the ship. The musketeers fired, but the swift canoes swept the waters like wings of birds, and gone was the wonderful Epenow, and gone were the Englishmen's hopes of finding caves of gold through the pilotage of the sharp-witted Indian captive.

"It made the Indians laugh to tell the story of how Epenow had got away.

"It was a sorry voyage that the English made on their return, without gold or treasure of any kind, and with the tale of how foolishly they had been outwitted.

"Fancy Sir Ferdinando when the news was brought to him! But the Indian was not more cunning and deceitful than had been his captors, and he had a right to be free, though not by such arts as these."

"Do you think that we will ever see Epenow?" asked little Ellen More. "I would be afraid of him."

"You are not unlikely to meet both Epenow and Tus-quanto; but were I Epenow, I would be very careful never to fall into the hands of the English again."

"I do not blame Epenow for what he did," said one of the boys. "I would have done the same. Such things must make the Indians look upon the traders as enemies. Deception does not pay."

"No, my lad," said the pilot. "They pay dearly who handle this coin, be they English or Indians."

"Is your story quite true?" asked Wrastle Brewster, one of the boys.

" Yes; in substance both the stories of Tusquanto and Epenow are true; you must allow a story-teller to use his imagination when that only serves to make a fact a picture."

Some four days were passed on the voyage to Southampton. There were spires rising in the sunset. Gables—the palace where Anne Boleyn spent her few happy days with Henry VIII.

Netley Abbey gleamed afar. Along the sea were great walls mantled with ivy. On the hills rose great clusters of oaks. Near by was the New Forest, and farther away lay Winchester with its cathedral, where were buried the early kings.

They were approaching the place where Canute ordered back the sea and it did not obey him.

They were in Southampton Water.

# CHAPTER VI.

THE heroes and saints of the world are those who build life the direct opposite of their natural character, on the principle that it is only that which is true that has any right to exist. The Leyden Pilgrims had learned this truth when they had given up wealth and the prospects of ease in age that they might live for the highest principles of the soul. Many of them had been men who had loved their own will, but had come to see that strength and power lie in giving up one's will for the good of a common cause.

The happy midsummer voyage from Leyden was over, and their troubles were now to begin. They had fallen into the hands of selfish, overbearing men, who were to carry them across the sea. They expected to go in two ships. The smaller of these was the Speedwell, Captain Reynolds, of which the pilot was good Robert Coppin. She was a pinnace, as we have said, without decks, of some sixty tons.

The larger ship was the Mayflower, Captain Jones, of which Christopher Martin was to be the governor for the company, and which awaited them on Southampton Water.

The voyage of the Speedwell from Delftshaven to
46

Southampton Water was full of promise.  But the little ship had been overmasted in Holland, a thing which will cause the timbers to spring at sea.  It has been claimed that this was purposely done, as Captain Reynolds had contracted to remain in the service of the colony a year, and wished to escape his obligation.  The charge may not have been well founded, but perilous times for the little Speedwell were at hand.

It was the purpose of the Pilgrims to have the Mayflower and Speedwell leave Southampton Water about August 1st, and they expected to arrive on the Hudson River in October, after a voyage in summer and early autumn weather.

They were not supposed to be sailing for Plymouth on the bleak New England coast, where the good Scottish pilot, Robert Coppin, had seen Indians, but for the sheltered shores of the Hudson, of which " our pilot " will have some stories to tell.

The overmasting of the Speedwell in Holland, causing her to leak as soon as she was out on the high sea, changed the whole plan of the voyage, and was the cause of great events, which had a powerful and far-reaching influence on the destiny of the American nation.    The hardships of New England were to school American life.

On a serene day in early August the two ships, the Mayflower, Captain Jones, and the Speedwell, Captain Reynolds, sailed out of Southampton Water, leaving behind the

beautiful views of the ivied walls and towers.   A part of
the Pilgrims were on the larger and a part on the smaller
ship.   The two ships sailed in view of each other, and everything indicated a prosperous voyage.   The young folks felt
secure, for " our pilot " was on board.

The Speedwell crowded on sail, and for a little time
made her name good.   But on the wide sea she began to
strain under the canvas, and the boards in her hull spread
apart, and it became hard to keep out the water.   The condition grew worse and worse.

" I must consult Captain Jones," said Captain Reynolds.
" The pinnace will soon fill with water and will sink.   We
can never cross the sea as we are now."

To the leaks we may fancy that Robert Coppin brought
the unwelcome jackscrew, and that the boys cheered when
they saw him about to apply the powerful *push* to a refrac-
tory beam.   The leak was stayed, and we may hear the
pilot say to Wrastle Brewster:

" Ho, my hearty! "

And the boys respond:

" Ho, my hearty! "

But a stayed leak may cause two leaks to open.   The
jackscrew could do much, but it could not overcome the
Atlantic Ocean.

" It is little use for a pinnace like this to contend against
the sea," said the pilot.   " We will have to go ashore again."

" You will not leave us? " said the boys.

" No, no; I have shipped for all the way."

Some of the boards sprung so that one could lay one's hand between them. It was useless to try to bail out the water; one might almost as well have tried to bail the ocean.

It was a bitter disappointment to the Pilgrims to find the little ship in this pitiful and perilous state.

" We must go back and repair," said Captain Reynolds to Captain Jones.

" It will cause us to arrive late on the Hudson," said Captain Jones. " But we must put back, or the pinnace will sink."

So the ship put back and anchored in Dartmouth Harbor, and the Speedwell was overhauled, and was made, as was supposed, seaworthy.

The two ships started out again, the Speedwell following close to the Mayflower, crowded with her sightly sails. But they had hardly gone a hundred leagues beyond Land's End when the Speedwell began to yawn and to leak again, and Captain Reynolds declared to Captain Jones that they must take back the ship or she would go to pieces. So the two ships went back again to the coast—this time to Plymouth. They unloaded the Speedwell, sent back twenty discouraged people to their homes, and with one hundred and two persons on board set sail for the Hudson, on the 6th of September; or, strangely enough, they set sail from Plymouth, England, to arrive in Plymouth, New England, for it was another power than their own that was directing their voyage.

What a sifting of people there had been to elect the heroes who were to make this voyage, in which human destiny was so greatly concerned! Macaulay said that God sifted the nations of the world to make the band of Pilgrim pioneers. Those who had lacked faith had been left behind in England; the aged had been left in Holland, and now those who had not the courage had been sent home.

One of the discouraged adventurers, Mr. Cushman, has left some account of the terrible days when the Speedwell was found leaking. You may like to read it—it is a picture.

" Our pinnace [, the Speedwell,] will not cease leaking; else, I think, we had been half way at Virginia. Our voyage hither hath been as full of crosses as ourselves have been of crookedness. We put in here to trim her; and I think, as others also, if we had stayed at sea but three or four hours more, she would have sunk right down. And though she was twice trimmed at [South]hampton; yet now she is as open and [as] leaky as a sieve: and there was a board, two feet long, a man might have pulled off with his fingers; where the water came in as at a mole hole.

" Friend, if ever we make a Plantation, GOD works a miracle! especially considering how scant we shall be of victuals; and, most of all, ununited amongst ourselves, and devoid of good tutors and regiment [leaders and organization]. Violence will break all. Where is the meek and humble spirit of MOSES? and of NEHEMIAH, who reedified the walls of Jerusalem, and the State of Israel? Is not the sound of REHOBOAM's brags daily heard amongst us? Have not the philosophers and all wise men observed that, even in settled Common Wealths, violent Governors bring, either themselves, or [the] people, or both, to ruin? How much more in the raising of Common Wealths, when the mortar is yet scarce tempered that should bind the walls?

"If I should write to you of all things which promiscuously forerun our ruin, I should overcharge my weak head, and grieve your tender heart: only this I pray you, Prepare for evil tidings of us, every day! But pray for us instantly [without ceasing]! It may be the Lord will be yet intreated, one way or other, to make for us. I see not, in reason, how we shall escape, even the gasping of hunger-starved persons: but GOD can do much; and his will be done!"

Such a man had not the inspiration for a voyage of the Argonauts. He went back among the discouraged twenty, as he should have done.

Robert Coppin brought with him the jackscrew from the Speedwell when he came on board the Mayflower for the last time.

The young folks, after all their terrors, cheered when they saw the jackscrew in his hand.

"It is shipped for all the voyage," he said, "like myself.

The ocean has beaten me once, but I will have a wrestle with her again."

"Cheer, cheer for Robert, our pilot," said Wrastle Brewster.

"Don't call me that," said the lusty sailor; "call me Bob. We'll get somewhere yet, by the aid of the jackscrew. It minds me that Providence only knows where we will land, but we will land somewhere."

And now the Mayflower is on the sea. It is the sixth of September. The weather is fair, but the season is getting late. In a few days or weeks they may expect the equinoctial gales.

Captain Jones was a hard, testy man. He domineered over the Pilgrims, and their governor insulted them with high words. But in the beautiful weather of the early days of the voyage he probably did not prevent "our pilot" from relating to the little Pilgrims his adventures in the New World.

England was gone, and the women and the children must have felt the influence of the kindly heart of "our pilot."

"Tell us new stories now that we are on the new ship," said little Ellen More.

"Once when I was in the woods," said the pilot, "I saw a little deer amid the cedars, and I made chase for it so as to get a range to shoot it for our meat.

"I followed it with an Indian trail, when what do you

think I saw? The animal suddenly went up into the air, and there it remained. I was amazed. I thought that it had fallen under the power of some Indian wizard, who, they say, work enchantment.

"But the deer in the air uttered a pitiful cry, and it touched my heart. I heeded the cry and went to it. Its head was hanging down in the air. Its eyes stood out of its head and its tongue was out of its mouth.

"It had been caught in an Indian snare. The Indians bend over the top of a birch tree and put a noose on it, and hold it to the ground by a wooden bar set in two notches in trees, so that it will slip out when a foot gets entangled in the noose and cause the tree to fly up. This snare had a powerful birch for its pole, and the deer was young and slender, and so was lifted into the air as by magic.

"I cut the noose, and it did look at me so pitifully that I let it go. One hates to kill an animal that he has released. We love everything that we help and hate everything that we injure. So we must love everybody and everything."

"Even Captain Jones?" asked the child.

The pilot did not answer. The wind was fair, the sky blue, and the ocean a long, rippling splendor, and such was the voyage for many days.

"Will you not tell us some stories of the Hudson, where we are going?" asked Ellen More.

"Aye, I will, if the weather continues fair," said "our

pilot," "and it may be like this all of the way. But the season is getting late, and it is storms I fear; I am preparing for storms; the time for them is at hand."

He told them tales of the sea birds. Captain Jones betimes gave him a harsh word, but he was used to such treatment on the sea.

"It is not the storms that I fear," said he, "it is the cross waves and the sickness that such water brings."

The Mayflower went on and on in the bright September days.

They were going, as they thought, to New Amsterdam, where the Dutch had a great plantation. They were to build up an independent English colony beside the Dutch colony. So when Pilot Robert promised to relate to the little Pilgrims some stories that he had heard in the shipping places of the colonist companies in London and in Holland, even profane Captain Jones did not object; he liked to hear such stories himself. He was looking for rough weather, and he did not object to his pilot's making merry a few idle hours when the ship was yet going fair.

There were some rough and reckless people on board, who had the ungovernable spirit of Captain Jones. Bradford, in his so-called Log of the Mayflower, relates a brief but vivid story of the career of one of these. He says, writing after the manner of the Puritans:

"And I may not omit here a special work of GOD's Providence. There was a proud and very profane young

man, one of the seamen; of a lusty able body, which made
him the more haughty. He would always be contemning the
poor people in their sickness, and cursing them daily with
grievous execrations, and [he] did not let [stop] to tell
them, That he hoped to help to cast half of them overboard
before they came to their journey's end; and to make merry
with what [property] they had.   And if he were by any
gently reproved, he would curse and swear most bitterly.

"But it please GOD, before they came half [the] seas
over, to smite this young man with a grievous disease; of
which he died in a desperate manner and so [he] was himself the first that was thrown overboard.   Thus his curses
light[ed] on his own head: and it was an astonishment to
all his fellows; for they noted it to be the just hand of GOD
upon him."

In this manner the Pilgrims viewed all of the events of
life.   They believed that Providence was their real pilot,
and that they were on the sea of destiny.   Every event that
happened they held to be ordered by God.   In all things
their faith was their anchor.   They were Argonauts sailing
not for themselves, but for the welfare of mankind.

# CHAPTER VII.

DAY after day the Mayflower moved on under heavy sail. The white wings of the birds that followed her far out of Southampton Water disappeared, and the New World's ark, the ship of the new Argonauts, was steadily piloted over the calm solitude of the waters toward the west.

Many of the passengers who had been sick in the early days of the voyage were well again. Governor Carver and his wife, Rose Standish and Elizabeth Winslow—how sad was the fate that awaited these lovely and gentle spirits!— might talk now of the nation that they hoped to found where the children would be educated in freedom of faith, and in which the ancient prophecies should be fulfilled.

We can fancy Elder Brewster repeating to them the ancient Jewish prophecy:

" A stone is about to be cut out of the mountain without hands, that will break into pieces all the other nations of the earth."

" But what will become of the Indian races? " said Elizabeth Winslow, whose heart loved every one and pitied all who were unfortunate.

"They will either become converted to God or will perish," said the elder. "They have been a bloody and revengeful race, and it may be their hour of salvation is come, or that their cup of iniquity is full."

"We must all labor to bring them to a knowledge of the truth," said the amiable lady. "Who do you think these races are, and how do you imagine that they found America?"

"I think, my lady, that they may be the descendants of the lost tribes of Israel. Or they may have been wanderers from the regions of the Nile across Asia in the days of the Shepherd Kings. Or they may be the descendants of some Mongolian race."

"How did they find America?"

"That would not have been difficult in the long gone days. The strait between Asia and America (Behring's) is not wide now, and it must once have been very narrow, and perhaps there was once no strait there at all. And nations wandering across Asia could have easily made the passage to America in boats."

"Oh," said Mistress Elizabeth, "if the Indians are the descendants of the lost tribes, and we could convert them, what a glorious voyage this would be! It makes my heart throb to think of it."

"One of two things," we imagine the prophetic Carver to have said, "will happen to these races. They will either give up their savagery or perish. That is the law of the human kind when a superior race mingles with a lower race."

"It was Robinson's wish that we might win the Indian races back to God.   Of this he dreams continually; for this he prays.   Oh, that he could have crossed the sea with us, and inspired us for this great work!"

"We are being guided by an unseen hand," said Carver. "But whether we are to found a new nation or to convert an old one we can not see; we can only know that whatever may happen, the law of righteousness will live, and those who obey it will rise and those who reject it may fall."

"Our people have not treated the Indian races well on their voyages," said Rose Standish.   "I hope we will follow the heart of Robinson in all that we do."

The October moon was on the sea.   The ship was drifting fair, and Robert Coppin, the pilot, came toward this group who were reviewing the thoughts of Elder John Robinson in regard to the conversion of the Indians, and listened to their hopes and plans.

The young people and children gathered around him. The little audience was almost a solid one, and they engaged in most earnest conversation as the ship's lights swayed under the moon and stars.

When the older people had ceased to talk in regard to the conversion of the Indians, Love Brewster said:

"Now let me ask 'our pilot' what he has heard in regard to the Hudson River, where we are going.   Pilot

Coppin, who was Henry Hudson, and how did he find the river where the Dutch have settled? We should surely know more of him."

To this inquiry Elder Brewster assented as one eminently proper to be made. Mistress Bradford, Mistress Standish, and Mistress Winslow seemed as interested in the question as the boys Jasper Richard More and Wrastle and Love Brewster. Mary Allerton and Priscilla Mullins sat side by side, eager to hear what Coppin would say. The whole company became silent, and under the moonlit sails Robert Coppin related the following strange story:

### CAST ADRIFT.

" It is a story to draw tears that I will tell you now.

" There was once a hardy sailor, and where he is now no one knows, be he living or dead. His name was, as you have already guessed, Henry Hudson, and he dreamed of making great discoveries in the north after the manner of those that had been made in the Spanish Main. His early life is a mystery, but he had one boy whom he dearly loved, and he took this boy wherever he went on his many voyages.

" He made many voyages, and those of them to the north had filled the shipping world with wonder. He prepared for a fourth voyage, on which he expected to find a polar sea.

" While dreaming of the lands he would discover, and that would make him rich and famous, he became acquainted

with a young man of most engaging manners but dissolute
habits, named Henry Greene.   The better class of people
had withdrawn from association with this false-hearted
youth, and even his own family had left him to his own
fate.

"The great navigator pitied him, and sought to reform
him.   He took him into his heart and his own home, and he
said to him one day:

"'Henry, go with me to the north.   You shall share in
the glory of the discoveries we will make, and on your return
I will report you to the crown and secure for you a place in
the royal service.'

"Henry Greene loved roystering and dissolute company,
but he was so abandoned by friends and fortune that he
accepted the invitation to sail to the mysterious countries
of the north, where the nights were long, where the ice
mountains glittered in the moon, where the northern
lights filled the sky with wonder.   So he made himself a
devoted friend of the captain, and Henry Hudson sailed
away for Greenland in April, some eleven years ago (1610),
with insufficient provisions, and he reached Greenland in
June.

"They came to a strait in the ice lands that led to an
inland sea (Hudson Bay).   Here was a land of desolation
and surprise.   But it was a land of winter and night, of
savage animals and lone Indians.

"The summer passed, and Hudson, having failed to find

a country that promised him wealth, proposed to his men to winter in the wild regions of darkness, ice, and snow.

"He was a quick-tempered man, although he so much loved his son and had taken such a friendly interest in the fascinating Henry Greene.

"The men rebelled at the thought of staying in the land of desolation, where there was neither wealth nor glory for them. They knew that their provisions were scanty, and there was but a poor prospect of hunting in the cold.

"'I will have to leave some of you behind,' said the irritable captain, when the men complained that the ship's provisions were getting low.

"The men began to plot against him, and among his secret enemies was Henry Greene.

"One day, when his friends were below decks, one of the conspirators closed the hatch and shut them down, and the mutineers at once seized the captain and bound him, and put him, with his son and some friends, among them a faithful carpenter, on board the shallop, which they had towed after the ship. They then formed a company of their own to sail the ship, and they made Henry Greene captain, and resolved to return immediately to England. That was a dark day when Henry Hudson, a man of noble parts, met Henry Greene.

"For a time the ship drew the shallop after her. Then came the fatal time to cut the rope. As they did so, the lost navigator heard a voice ringing through the air that pierced his heart.

"It was that of the villain, Henry Greene!

"Henry Greene, captain, sailed away, leaving the shallop rocking on the icebound sea, with only provisions for a few days. Whatever became of Henry Hudson we do not know. Ships were sent out to find him, but he was never seen. He probably has perished amid the ice, he and his faithful son.

"But we do know what became of the faithless Henry Greene. He landed on the coast for provisions, and was set upon by the natives and murdered.

"The survivors undertook to take the ship home. Their provisions failed, and when they came to Iceland they were too weak to walk the decks. They told their tale. So all of these people who were engaged in plans to cast others adrift were themselves cast adrift on the sea and on the world.

"But it was this same Henry Hudson, with his faithful boy, who discovered the land for which we are now sailing, and which they call New Amsterdam. He passed through raging waters [Hell Gate] and came to a most beautiful bay, and sailed up a river through a land of plenty, which we may find, and have better luck than he. The best thing that can be said of any man is that he is true-hearted, and all who are will have the heartache some day in this troubled world.

"It is a hard and lonesome story."

" Is it the Hudson River that was found by the captain whom they cast adrift in the ice to which we are going? " said little Ellen More to our pilot, as he sat with a very troubled and far-away look in his face.

" Ah! child, ah! child, you may well ask me that. Older heads might think that question. I wonder myself if we shall find ourselves there at last."

The child was startled at the strange look in the pilot's face. She laid her white hand on his rough palm and said:

" It may be that we will go to the country of the great and good Indian king of whom you spoke. It may be that we are carrying the copper chain to him. It makes me feel glad to think of it. How I should like to see him wearing it with a pleased look! And all under the greenwood trees. Do you think I will, Pilot Coppin? "

The pilot smiled and then he shuddered.

The Mayflower was carrying a dark secret in the head of her captain which it is probable that only the pilot suspected. His suspicion, were it so, would not have troubled him had not his heart turned toward the Pilgrims in their high purpose, struggles, and sufferings.

Was the Mayflower really bound for the Hudson River?

Only Captain Jones and the planters of the Dutch colonies in England and Holland really knew. But the

pilot would know some day.   There would come to him
a secret order from Captain Jones that would disclose to
him his real purpose.   So under a dark secret were they
crossing the sea; the angel of Providence was still in all
events.

# CHAPTER VIII.

THE serene days passed, and cross waves began to shake the ship and to cause a renewal of seasickness among the passengers. The blue sky became overcast and wild, sullen under clouds drifted across the wide gray canopy of cloud that shut out the sun.

Storms were approaching. One of them struck the ship in such a manner as to cause her to strain and tremble. The waves became higher and higher. The sea rolled green and white under a dim gray light.

The Mayflower was in the middle of the great ocean, and a hundred times a day seemed to be lost as she sank into the trough of the sea.

The first storm was succeeded by another. The rain fell in sheets and the nights were blackness. The wind lashed the waves. It seemed impossible that the ship could ever survive the war of the elements that raged on every side.

"O pilot," said Rose Standish, "did you ever see weather like this before?"

"Many a time, lady."

"Did the ship live?"

"You may comfort your heart when I tell you that she did."

"We are but a speck in infinity," said Mistress Bradford, "and I do not feel that I shall ever rest my foot on the land again. But what matters it if you may live to carry the Gospel to the Indians? I have ceased to care for myself."

Storm followed storm. One day Captain Jones said to the pilot:

"We can not bear a bit of sail; we shall be forced to hull" (to drift without sails).

The days when the ship was in hull were terrible indeed. All felt their helplessness. The women cried; the children gathered in a pitiful group and cried out:

"O pilot, when will this weather be over?"

"Keep up your courage, my hearties. I have weathered storms as hard as these. You shall live to see sunny skies again, and great oak forests, and Indian kings. Heaven holds her own in her hands, and John Robinson's prayers have not gone up to heaven in vain. Trust, trust, trust!"

Poor little Ellen More clung to the pilot wherever he went, even at the wheel.

"I am all alone," she said; "you do pity me, don't you? I am all alone in the world and on the sea."

"It is the Mistress Winslow that is good to ye," said the pilot. "She is good to everybody. You must cling to her, and not to a poor rover like me."

" But, pilot, I love you."

" Love me, love me, Ellen More? Oh, that these dull old ears should ever hear that. O my little girl, that goes right to my heart, and while Robert Coppin lives you shall never want for a friend. Little Ellen More, I would die for such as thou."

" O Master Coppin, do you say that? Suppose we were to go down?"

" Then I will go down with thee in my arms. What am I?—a poor sailor! What is life to me? I am not sent to convert the Indians. I would love to die for such a heart as yours, Ellen More."

" You will let me cling to you, won't you?"

" Yes, yes, my darling heart. This old pilot will let you do that—he will now."

" At the wheel?"

" Yes, at the wheel."

" And if I should die, you tell me the way I must go. Pilot, pilot, you will tell me the way."

" O Ellen More, Ellen More, this breaks my heart. But I will be true to the wheel. If a true heart will bring us to land, you will see the light of the shore again. Living or dying, I will be true to thee, Ellen More."

" And I will cling to thee, Pilot Robert—let me call you that—you are our pilot."

" No, no, child."

" Then who is?"

"God.   He holds the waters in the hollow of his hand."

As the ship lay in hull, drifting sailless and helpless, a great wave dashed over her, and the cry arose:

"John Howland has gone overboard!"

"Overboard! a man overboard!" passed from lip to lip.

"John Howland is overboard!" cried the captain.

The ship was rolling from side to side.   One could see but a little way ahead, for everywhere in a dim light rose the billows.

John Howland, who was in the service of Governor John Carver, was a strong, lusty young man, one of the last of the passengers who would seem likely to meet with any accident.

He had come above the gratings when the ship was rolling and the waves dashing above the decks, and had been thrown into the sea.

"John Howland is overboard!" said little Ellen More to the pilot, in terror.   "You save him, oh do!"

The topsail halyards hung over the helpless ship and out into the water.

John Howland went down some fathoms under the waves, but he was buoyed up, and, strange as it may seem, caught hold of the dragging halyards under the sea, and his strong arm held to them with a grasp like death.

The pilot saw that the halyards were shaken by a power under the waves.

"Haul up the halyards, gently, gently, for Heaven's sake, gently, man!"

He seized the ropes.

They drew up the halyards. John Howland came up with them. The pilot shouted as he saw the young man's head.

"Saved!" he cried. "Pass the word. John Howland is saved! It is a miracle."

They drew John Howland up into the ship by a boat hook.

"But for the halyards I should have perished," said the young man.

"But for the providence of God you would have perished," said Elder Brewster.

They carried him below and laid him down. The shock left him with but little strength and he fell ill.

"John Howland, a good spirit was with thee in the storm," said the pilot. "You will recover, and will see the light of land. May be that you will live to tell your grandchildren of this strange event; may be you will."

Calmer weather came under colder skies. The women shrank from the chill. The children felt the bitter weather, all except little Ellen More. She tented under the great sea coat of Pilot Robert, and helped him with brace and wheel to direct the rudder to the gray west.

November was now on the ocean. One of the passengers, William Butler, in the service of Dr. Samuel Fuller, we think, **fell very sick.** He longed to see the new land,

and the heart of all went out to him as he lay in his bunk day by day, tossed by the dark agitated sea.

One morning a deep silence fell upon all.

"It is over," said Dr. Fuller to our pilot. "You must do your office."

They wrapped the body in the scanty clothing he had brought in his chest.

Then Elder Brewster knelt down beside the dead, and the sublime words of Hebrew psalmody, "Lord, thou hast been our dwelling-place in all generations," rose amid the storm.

Our pilot took up the body gently and laid it in the great graveyard of the deep, and as it sunk from sight forever all bowed in tears, and heard the elder's voice saying:

"Until the deep gives up its dead!"

# CHAPTER IX.

In these troubled days of the equinox, the cross seas, and the long-continued fall storms, the captain was one day seen to be in an unusually ugly and profane mood. He called to him the ship's carpenter and stormed at him, then the pilot, and talked to him in a high tone. One of his exclamations rose above the winds. It was:

" If it can not be replaced we shall all go down, and the ranters will go with us. That is all."

Some of the Pilgrims, many of whom were lying on their beds, which were soaked with the dashing of the sea, heard these ominous words and started up. The dismal exclamation of Captain Jones was passed from one to another, and when it reached little Ellen she said:

" Then I will never live to give the copper chain to the red forest king. But Pilot Robert, he can save us. A soul like his has power with God." A great sea dashed upon the ship, and the water came over the decks.

Edward Winslow went to the pilot, seeing that the captain was in no mood to be questioned.

6

"Pilot, what was it that the captain said? That the ship was in danger?"

"The ship is straining, sir, and there is a leak. The main beam has sprung out of place."

Edward Winslow went back to the men of the Mayflower.

"The ship," said he, "is straining from stem to stern. Even our pilot says that we are in danger."

"What shall we do? Shall we have to return?" asked many voices.

The captain came below.

"Is the ship in danger?" asked Elder Brewster.

"In danger? Well, I should say she was. The main beam is sprung, and the men are toiling at the pumps. What a miserable expedition all this is!"

"Would you advise us to return?" asked the governor of the ship, who was the adviser of the Pilgrims.

"No!" thundered the captain. "It is as far from here to England as it is to America. We will go on or go down. We would be as likely to go down in an attempt to return as we would to go on. No, no, whistle, ye winds, and dash over us, ye seas! We will go on or down, and it is down that we will go unless the beam can be forced into place again."

Many of the women—the Pilgrim mothers—were sick, but they started up and began to pray and to talk in the language of faith to each other.

The waves rolled high, and the ship quivered, and the leak grew. There were faith, terror, brave words, and faltering lips among the little nation sitting by their sea-soaked beds in the dim light below. Sea after sea smote the windward side of the ship. The frail bark seemed as a thistle down in a November hurricane.

For hours the terror lasted. Night came, a darkness of death. Few dared to sleep.

The gray morning rose over the ocean. The sailors were worn out, and hope seemed to have fled.

At last the Pilgrims heard a firm step on the stairs. There was faith in it, and it was coming down. The men lifted their hands when they saw who it was. The women cried out and wept.

"Robert Coppin, our pilot," said Elizabeth Winslow, "can you save the ship?"

"Pilot Robert, you have come to be our Moses," said Rose Standish. "I can feel it, I can feel it."

"God help you to save us," cried Mistress Carver.

A child's voice rose above the rest.

"He will! he will!"

It was Ellen More.

The pilot bent his face, full of love and pity, on the child.

"I will do everything human power can for you, my girl."

"The chief must have the copper chain," said she.

"Aye, aye, and I have seen as dark a stress of weather as this, but never a ship so strained in mid-ocean."

A new resolution seemed to come to him with the words of the child and the vision of the copper chain.

He suddenly put his hand to his head and exclaimed:

"Thank God!"

"What?" asked many voices.

"The jackscrew, boys, where is the jackscrew? Bring me the jackscrew!"

They brought the curious instrument out of the baggage; he seized it and rushed toward the broken rib of the ship, crying, "Send the ship's carpenter to me!"

He applied the power of the screw to the beam, or rib, which had been wrenched from its place. The ship's carpenter joined him at once, and Wrastle and Love Brewster stood by him and a crowd gathered around him.

The captain came roaring down and cleared the boys away.

"A jackscrew!" cried one of the officers. "A jack straw might answer as well."

"But the beam is moving back," said the pilot.

"Then," said the officer, "the Power that uplifted the arm of Moses must be in it; if you can do that you can do more than old Canute did when he ordered back the sea."

But the beam moved. Slowly, and at times it obeyed the power applied, when the ship righted and the beam was lifted into its place.

"The beam does not spring back," said the pilot, "and I move it into place a little every time the ship rights."

Hour by hour he applied the jackscrew, and the captain and the officers of the ship and the Pilgrim company came and stared as they saw Robert Coppin and the ship's carpenter overcoming the elements and the adverse forces of gravitation, until the rib of the ship stood firm again.

At last the pilot started up.

"Wrastle Brewster," said he, "go and tell little Ellen More that the Mayflower is safe! It was not the jackscrew—no, no, it was a Power behind the jackscrew that guided us and has provided for us. Providence has ordered that the Pilgrim company shall build an everlasting habitation of faith and freedom beyond the sea!"

They came to calmer waters.

The Indian summer weather, so beautiful upon the land, sends its influence far out to sea.

One day the captain said to Pilot Robert:

"We must run landward soon. Steer hard toward the west."

"Captain, it is the Hudson River for which we are booked to sail."

"Pilot Robert Coppin, don't you dare to reply to me or to ask me any questions. It is your office to obey, and not to reason aloud or to argue with any one. I know my business, sir. Steer hard toward the west."

" You surely are not deceiving these poor people? "

" The people's affairs are no part of your duties, sir. Steer toward the west. If we shall touch upon the Plymouth country what is that to you? You are to obey me, sir, and to ask no questions. I have given you great liberties in this voyage, and these people seem to have brought you over to them. They did not employ you; it was I, and I know what I am doing, and do not want and will never receive any unasked-for advice from any inferior officer. So not one word more. Cease you story-telling; stop all this association with women and children. Attend in the future strictly to your own duties, and bear toward the west! "

Robert Coppin, pilot, had probably expected such an order. He understood it. It was in his contract to obey the captain and not to follow his own sense of equity, of the truth of which he could not be sure.

But to " bear hard to the west " would take the ship to a long sandy cape in Massasoit's country, before it could come to the Hudson River. That cape was known as Malebar and also as Cape Cod.

What was the captain's purpose in prolonging the journey amid the wintry seas?

Had he been bribed by the Dutch to keep away from their rich territory at Manhattan?

If so, no one on board but the pilot could have suspected it at this time.

So the Mayflower goes on her way over the troubled waters.

There is a white wing in the sky. A sea bird appears. The pilot bears hard to the west!

Beside the jackscrew there were other things that the Pilgrims were bringing over the sea that excited the interest of all in the days of quiet water. Elizabeth Winslow had a curious mortar and pestle. Where would it find use?

Mistress Brewster had a looking-glass, into which it was the delight of the young people to see their faces. It was taken out of the chest at times and passed around, and was very carefully handled. It answered the question:

"How do I look now?"

Mistress Elizabeth Winslow had a very beautiful figured mat, which was like a picture to unroll. It was green.

"It is fine enough for a king," said Pilot Coppin one day when Mistress Winslow had unrolled it. "The Indian kings sit down on the ground when they are in council. Perhaps we shall hold a council with an Indian chief some day. If so, we would want that mat."

"The Indian chief smokes in his council," said John Billington, the boy. "Perhaps *he* would want your silver pipe."

"That is a point well taken, my boy. But I would be slow to give away the pipe that the Traders' Company gave to me. Let me go to get the pipe."

It was in the few calm days of the latter part of the voyage. The people seemed all to fall into the spirit of amusing and entertaining each other.

So Mistress Brewster brought out the looking-glass and laid it down on the famous chest on which the compact would one day be signed, and the sea-worn people looked into it to see " how they looked now."

Mistress Brewster spread out the green rug before the chest, and Pilot Coppin came bringing the silver pipe, which was his special treasure, it having been given him for faithful service on the high seas.

Others brought out litle keepsakes and treasures, and related the simple history of them.

John Billington had a quick fancy. He began to tell little Ellen More a fairy story: how that the mat would some day be unrolled under the oaks of Virginia, and a great king, with fur robes and feathers and pearl shells, would come and sit upon it, and smoke the silver pipe.

Ellen, too, was a child of imagination, and she called Pilot Coppin to hear the wonderful tale that John had told.

" Strangely enough," he said, " such dreams as these come true. The soul's purpose is in them and behind them. I believe in fairy stories, though others do not. There is good suggestion in them. The world is governed by suggestion."

" Say you that, Pilot Coppin? " asked Elder Brewster.

"Yes, yes, think of the power of the suggestion in the parable of the prodigal son!"

"You may be right, Pilot Coppin. I had not thought of life in that way, but I will take a look at it so. You are a very hopeful man. A ship needs a hopeful man for a pilot."

"So does the ship of life, Elder Brewster; one that would say good cheer if a boat were going to pieces on the waves, and in that spirit the chances are that we would not be lost."

Whales were seen spouting in these days of calmer water. The ship drove on and on, into the sunlight, into the shade, into the red morning, into the pale starlight, into the night.

Whither go they? The sails are the wings of destiny. Whither go they? The nation of nations is on the sea. On and on.

On and on. Will the mat ever be spread for an Indian king, or the copper chain given to chief or sagamore? On and on!

# CHAPTER X.

THE Pilgrims were long making preparations for their journey, and they crowded into their baggage many strange and curious things beside the copper chain and the jewel to give to some great forest lord. Some of these curious things are still to be found in old houses in the cape towns and elsewhere among Puritan descendants.

Among these interesting relics none is more wonderful than Miles Standish's sword, which may still be seen in Pilgrim Hall in Plymouth.

When the seas began to run smoother again, the boys and girls of the Mayflower importuned Robert Coppin for stories in the idle hours.

Who were the boys and girls of the Mayflower? It was the colonization plan of Robinson, of Leyden, that the young people should sail first for the founding of a new colony, and that the older people should follow them. He himself expected to join them in the New World when the fathers of the Pilgrim republic should sail, but he did not live to follow them. The pilot of the Argo of old did not return, and the prophets of great movements do not often live to see them fulfilled, except in faith and promise.

When we look at the names of the boys and girls of the Mayflower, it would seem that they were a large part of the company of that ship of destiny. One wonders as one reads it.

There were Jasper More and William Latham, two boys in the service of John Carver, the first governor. Jasper More died in Cape Cod harbor.

There were Love Brewster and Wrastle, or Wrestling, Brewster, two sons of Elder Brewster, and Richard More and his brother, in the same family.

There was Ellen More in the Winslow family. She was a sister of the boys of the same name. The More children were orphans.

There were Bartholomew Allerton, Remember and Mary Allerton, and John Hooke, a servant boy in the Allerton family.

There were Joseph Mullins, a child, and the famous Priscilla Mullins, a girl, in the Mullins family.

There was Resolved White. Peregrine White was born on board of the Mayflower.

There were Giles Hopkins and Constance Hopkins, and three more children of the Hopkins name. Oceanus Hopkins was born on the Mayflower.

There were two boys in the Billington family, John and Francis.

There were Henry Samson and Humility Cooper, both children in the Tilley family, and John Tilley and Elizabeth Tilley, a son and daughter.

There were Mary Chilton, Joseph Rogers, and John Cooke, and a son in the Tinker family; Samuel Fuller and two boys by the name of Turner. There were Samuel Eaton, a baby, and several young people in the service of the principal families.

There were thirteen children of the leading Pilgrims on board, and most of these were boys. Nobly enough, the Pilgrims brought their adopted children, or the children of their charity, with them.

There were more than twenty young people on board the ship, and to these "our pilot," who had seen Indians and gazed on the wonderful shores and fishing grounds of the new land, became more and more interesting; his heart drew them all to him; he was "Sinbad the Sailor" to these young emigrants.

Miles Standish was the man of valor among the company. Of him the young people must have stood in awe.

But one day when the sun was struggling through the clouds and the waves were merciful, the boys, among whom were the Brewsters, ventured to look at Miles Standish's sword.

It was a very curious sword. It had an inscription on it that no one could read. The emblems of the sun, moon, and stars were stamped upon it.

"That is a strange sword that you have, Master Standish," ventured Wrastle Brewster, who was young and bold.

"Would you like to see it bend?"

"Aye, aye, Master Standish!" cried the boys.

The stout man bent the sword and said:

"A Damascus blade, or like it."

"Where did it come from?" asked Richard More.

"From the air!"

The boys' eyes were filled with surprise.

"There are mines in the air as well as on the earth," said Standish. "This sword is said to have been made of meteoric metal."

"When was it made?" asked Wrastle Brewster.

"A thousand years ago, it may be," said the sturdy man, flashing it in a sunbeam. "In the days of Charlemagne, or of Peter the Hermit, or of the Crusades. I do not know when it was made. It is claimed that it was once a magic sword, but the charm upon it does not extend to me. I have nothing to do with any heathenish enchantments."

"What is engraved upon it?" asked Mary Allerton.

"*That* John Robinson, with all his learning, was not able to tell. An old man in Amsterdam poked it over with his long nose, and said that those were magic words to protect a devotee from evil. But I am no devotee to the faith of the pagans for which the charm was wrought. My protection comes only from my faith, honor, and courage."

"Where did you get it?" asked little Ellen More, as Robert Coppin lifted her up above the heads of those who were crowding close to the rugged Standish.

"Now why did you ask that, little girl? That is a secret, a story."

"Tell us the story, Master Standish," said Ellen More. "Pilot Coppin tells us stories. Do stories hurt any one?"

"No, no, my little girl. It is Coppin's little girl you seem to be—he has made you that by stories. Stories are fairy lands to such as you—well, never mind, the world is governed by imagination. I might refuse the boys, but I could never refuse such as you; marry, I could not. Well, here is the story of the sword, and an old one it is. Sit down and you shall hear!"

The short, stout, ruddy man turned the sword upward, as saluting on parade.

"I was once, as you know," he said, "a soldier in the Netherlands. Ears, all, and be quiet while I speak. In those days we were in Ghent, and one day I beheld a company of soldiers about to capture a girl who was out on some errand in the streets. I protected the girl, and enabled her to return safely home.

"Her father was an old armorer. He was very grateful to me for what I had done, for his daughter seems to have been all the world to him. So one day he made his way to me. He had something under his silk mantle. Ears all, now, and be quiet while I am talking.

"'I want to speak with you in private,' said he. 'Is any one around?'

"'No one, sir,' said I.

"He began to unfold his silken scarf or mantle.

"'You saved my daughter,' said he. 'I have brought a little present to you—not much to look upon, but it is the most precious gift I have. It came from the skies.'

"He drew back the mantle fold by fold, and the sword appeared.

"'Meteor metal,' said he. 'Damascus, and it has a grand legend, one worthy to make it sacred to a man of honor.'

"He held it aloft, looking around to see that no one was approaching.

"'What is the legend?' I asked, and motioned him to sit down.

"He sat down. An animation as of youth came into his withered face. How intense and how grateful he looked, that old armorer of Ghent!

"He said that when he was a young man he went to the East to engage in the war against the Turks, to bear the Cross against the Crescent. He was taken prisoner, and was carried into an Ottoman town, and there was cared for by a very beautiful young woman. She came to love him, and she told him of her love; but he said to her that there was one whom he loved and who loved him in his own land, and that to be a true man to all good people his heart must be true to her. Then the young woman loved him because his heart was true to the woman in the West, and to show him her respect for his honor she gave him this sword, which she said had been used in the Persian wars, and had a magic power to protect any man of honor from harm. Ears, all; be still while I speak. My honor shall protect me from harm, and this sword shall guard my honor, and the sword of Standish shall not only protect me from harm but you from harm, my little Ellen, and all you boys and girls from harm if you are ever in peril. It shall be drawn in honor for you all."

"I shall never fall into harm," said little Ellen More, "because I am carrying to the chief the copper chain. The red chiefs do not harm those who carry them presents."

"No, no," said John Alden, "and gifts from the heart are more powerful for good than swords."

The sun was still struggling among the clouds, and the sea was growing rough again. A wild night followed. The next morning at daybreak came a cry from a sailor, perhaps in the rigging.

"Land! I see land!"

They rushed to the deck.

Captain Jones was standing on deck staggering against a breeze, but with a broad smile on his face.

"I see land!" said Robert Coppin, shading his eyes.

"Where?" said Ellen More.

" There! " answered Coppin, pointing; " there, in the gray light."

" That is a cloud," said Mary Allerton.

" No, no, my girl, a cloud lies not low like that. I can see it glint. Look at the flocks of birds flying low there."

" And the whales," said Ellen; " one, two, three! "

" Back, children, back," said Pilot Coppin, " and leave me to my duty now."

There was great excitement on board. The sun disappeared, another storm was overhanging the sea.

But this was not the Hudson River, it was Cape Cod.

The ship plowed on under heavy sail, with rough waters before it. Several passengers were sick, and the cry of land set their pulses to beating again.

" I wish that it were here we were to land," said several of the men as the clouds lowered above them, and these men were sailors.

Nearer and nearer drew the ship to the land. The captain was advised to seek shelter here.

Land! But there was no one to welcome them; no houses, no warm inns, no hospitable roofs of any kind.

Winter was near. The trees were bending in the keen winds of the north.

Wild men were there, wild beasts. The shores were beaten by storms.

Mystery was there, an unknown destiny for those who would make that land their home.

7

But freedom was there; men there might own themselves, might hope, and trust, and live, and seek one another's welfare beyond the world of prisons and chains.

"Land!" The sound was glorious. Land where men could be free! Should they find rest here, or should they seek to go farther?

It is a common story now that Captain Jones had been bribed by the foreign traders with the Dutch colony on the Hudson to betray and deceive the Pilgrims, and to land them on the shores of Cape Cod. This may have been so, but it is not proved. We like to think that Captain Jones was an honest man.

The breaking of the storm revealed a fine harbor and shores covered with rugged oaks, sweet woods, and evergreens. The country seemed to invite the exiles to stop here, and the sea to forbid them to go farther.

The late fall storms off the coast were terrible, and Robert Coppin, "our pilot," spoke favorably of the land, which he had seen under different skies and in milder seasons. The influence of the pilot must have been very great at this time.

So the 11th of November found the Pilgrim company at Provincetown (Malabar or Malebar) Bay.

Little Ellen More began to talk of the green mat and the copper chain again.

# CHAPTER XI.

THE shores were goodly to behold. The land was much as now, except that the giant trees are now gone. There were green junipers there, mingled with sassafras. The ground was carpeted with prince's pine. The witch-hazels, which bloom in the fall, were there, and probably the red berries of the checkerberry among the creeping Jenny. However the latter may have been, wild fowl filled the coves, and fish sported in the shallow waters.

Whales were there in the deep waters. Robert Coppin, who was an experienced fisherman, was much excited when he saw what a harvest of the sea was there. "Our master and his mate," says a relation, "professed that we might have made £3,000 or £4,000 worth of all."

"We found great mussels," says the relation, "very fat and full of sea pearls, but the company could not eat them without being made sick. They caused even the sailors to cast them up."

The water was very shallow near the shore, so that those who landed had to wade, and in freezing weather.

Were they to land here and to seek for a place of settle-

ment, or to put out to sea again? They decided to give up
for the present the Hudson River plan, and to look for a
place of home making here.

But they must have a government here. What should
it be?

If all were to obey it, it must be founded on the votes
of the majority. The will of the majority must be the
new king in this empty land. But they must have officers
to execute this will. Who should they be? What should
they be called? They must have a governor and council.

How should the will of a majority of the people be
made known? By an election.

The new state must have a constitution or agreement.
The agreement must be one that a majority of the people
would sign. It must be a compact, such as is the Constitution of the United States to-day, which the people pledge
themselves to support before they can vote.

There is an old chest to be seen pictured in Pilgrim Hall
in Plymouth, on which a compact was probably written, and
studied, and signed. The original chest is in the keeping of
the Connecticut Historical Society. This compact was the
first constitution of a republic in the New World, and all of
the republics of the Western world have followed its princi-
ciple of self-government. The Declaration of Independence as a seed was in it. The Constitution of the United
States as a beginning was in it. The fall of the Bastile and
the French Constitution in a prophetic sense were in it.

*Reading the compact in the Mayflower's cabin.*

That simple paper on Elder Brewster's chest, if the legend of the chest may be trusted,\* was to bring a new order of government into the world. Destiny was to say to its spindles, " Thus forever go on! "

What a day that was, the 21st of November, N. S. It should be celebrated everywhere, in all lands where freedom by self-government is now, and as long as freedom through self-government shall last.

See Elder Brewster as he considers that paper with the rest. Did he dream of what he was doing? There were forty-one adult men on board; would they all sign it, or would some of them object to signing it?

The leaders must read it to all, then they must question all, and every one who agreed to sign this paper would give to the Pilgrim Constitution his vote.

One by one, as he listened to the reading said, " I will sign it." Forty-one said, " I will sign it." The charter of agreement was unanimously adopted. The first republic of America was founded in the cabin of the Mayflower, amid lowering skies and foaming seas.

What was the compact? Let the young reader not skip it, but read it. Every word is gold:

*In the name of GOD, Amen. We, whose names are underwritten, the loyal subjects of our dread Sovereign*

---

\* The proof that the lid of the chest was used for the purpose is wanting, but such seems to have been the tradition.

*Lord King JAMES; by the grace of GOD, of Great
Britain, France, and Ireland King; Defender of the
Faith; &c.*

*Having undertaken for the glory of GOD, and ad-
vancement of the Christian faith, and honour of our King
and country, a Voyage* [Expedition] *to plant the first Colony
in the northern parts of Virginia;* [we] *do, by these presents, solemnly and mutually, in the presence of GOD and
one of another, covenant and combine ourselves together into
a Civil Body Politic, for our better ordering and preserva-
tion; and furtherance of the ends aforesaid: and, by
virtue hereof, to enact, constitute, and frame such just and
equal laws, ordinances, acts, constitutions, Offices, from time
to time, as shall be thought most meet and convenient for the
general good of the Colony; unto which, we promise all due
submission and obedience.*

*In witness whereof, we have hereunder subscribed our
names. Cape Cod, 11th of November, in the year of the
reign of our Sovereign Lord King JAMES, of England,
France and Ireland 18; and of Scotland 54.* Anno Dom-
ini 1620.

Would you like to see how some of these signatures
looked?—signatures of more value to mankind than those
of the emperors of Rome in their purple, or of monarchs of
the middle ages in their pomp and power, signatures whose
importance did not cease with the death of the signers, but
remained a force unto this day in the advance of humanity.

HANDWRITING OF THE PILGRIMS.

Like John Hancock's signature to the Declaration of Independence, these names are penned in a bold, strong hand. By it each man became a king in the will of all the rest and his own. That was a glorious day for America. They elected John Carver governor. In that election the folkmote, or town meeting, was begun, and the folkmote was the pattern of the future republic.

A grand scene followed that poets should sing, musicians set to the music of the waves, and painters spread upon canvas.

After sixty-three days at sea they were now to land.

They must wade a "bow's length" or more in the cold,

shallow waters. So in the ship's boat the leaders came to the shore.

The pines welcomed them, the birch, the holly, the ash, the mossy oaks, the carpet of evergreen. Faith welcomed them in the air unseen.

They fell upon their knees. That was the first public thanksgiving in New England—it was on Compact Day. They faced the future by faith.

The people of Provincetown have been considering the celebration of this day. They should do so, and call to it the nation's noblest men. The whole country should join with them in the memory of an event that must ever rank foremost among the heroic and prophetic deeds of the world.

They at first found no human being in the open woods— no print on the sand, no abandoned homes or cabins, no tombs. The place was but one of the vast solitudes of the sea. The inhabitants of the land had nearly all been swept away by a plague a few years before.

On Monday, 13th of November, O. S., they unshipped their shallop and drew her to the land for the ship's carpenter to repair. It took many days to make the boat seaworthy. In the meantime they would explore the coast in a smaller boat, and would go inland to see if any people could be found.

As they returned at night from the first landing they brought pine or juniper boughs to burn on board the ship.

These boughs made a bright fire and filled the room with a resinous odor as they were burned.

How cheerful must have been the fire in the cabin of the Mayflower on that lonely night amid the rolling seas and the tenantless woods!

"Robert Coppin," said Ellen More, "you are to go out with the men and explore. Will you not tell us what you discover, on the evening after you return from exploring? The boys and girls will all want to hear. They will not let us go. Bring more juniper, and tell us about all that you shall see in the woods, by the green boughs as they burn."

"That I will, my darling girl—that Robert Coppin will."

"And you will have eyes for us?"

"Yes, yes, Robert Coppin will be eyes for you."

"And ears?"

"Yes, yes, and ears, Ellen More, Ellen More. I love the young folks on the Mayflower; my heart beats with theirs, and it will be a dark day to me when I leave them."

"May be that you will come back to us some day, Robert Coppin."

"Ah, if you were my little girl I would come back to you, but you have better friends than I can ever be to you, and it is my lot to roam the sea." He added, "But I shall never forget this voyage."

"The storms?" asked Ellen.

" Ah, no, not the storms, but the hearts in the storms. There have been hearts in the storms."

" Your heart has been in the storms," said Ellen. " Pilot Coppin, Pilot Coppin, it will all be well if you only lead us where we are to go. I would love to suffer if it would make happy such a heart as yours."

" Ellen More, Ellen More, I would die for such a one as you, but the world will pass us both by. What is a pilot? It may be for those who do their duty there is some better world than this. But the sailor must do his duty, and be forgotten. He is one wave of the ocean that comes up and sinks down again."

" But the ocean must have that one wave, Robert Coppin."

" Thou hast well said, my girl. It will make my heart beat faster to think each day when I am on land that I will return to tell my adventures to the boys and girls of the Mayflower and to you, Ellen More, who will ever have a warm place in my lonely heart."

# CHAPTER XII.

## THE FIRST DISCOVERY.

THE return of Pilot Coppin after the men had made their first expedition inland was hailed by all who had remained on board as a matter of intense interest. He came to tell a tale by the not unlikely juniper fire. He doubtless brought them Indian corn, parched acorns, and nuts, for such he had found in abundance, and it was his habit to share what most pleased him with others.

It is night on the Mayflower, a calm night now, under the moon and stars. The fire burns brightly and the lamps low. The men who have been on land, except Coppin, go to their bunks, weary with their hard journey.

Pilot Coppin sits down in the cabin among the women and the boys and girls. John Billington makes trouble in getting into a place to hear the tale of the first adventure. He was a boy who, we may fancy, was always making trouble by his restlessness. He had his father's temperament, a man who, although he discovered the Billington Sea, was hanged in 1630; so even the good Pilgrims had a bad man among them, whom their example failed to restrain.

" Hear ye, hear ye all! " began Pilot Coppin, using an ancient form of arresting attention, " and I will tell you the tale of our first adventures in the woods.

" The woods—you should see them!  They stand open like arcades; one could ride through them.  They must be beautiful in summer.  The blue jays, the wonder birds, that always come peeking about, are there now, with their feather caps on that bob up and down.  There are ospreys' nests in the dead trees and crows' nests in the pines.  There are withered flowers and red berries everywhere.

" Hear ye, hear ye all!  What day is this?—the 17th of November.  The first thing we saw as we went into the woods was, marching in single file, six Indians with a dog, coming in the direction that we were traveling."

" Indians! " cried the boys.  The pilot bade them be silent.

" You should have seen how surprised they were when they saw us.  They gave a cautious, mysterious whistle to the dog, and turned on their heels, as though they had seen the Evil One himself, and their dark heels flew like drumsticks in a battle.  How they did run!  They vanished. What do you suppose their thoughts could have been on seeing our faces, our armor, and our guns?  The dog did not stop to defend them; he caught their fear, and made off with them without stopping so much as to turn to bark.

" We hurried on after them, calling out, ' Ho, here, ho! '

Our voices must have caused them greater terror than before.

"We next saw them on top of a hill, looking down to watch the bushes move as we pressed on our way.

"We called, 'Ho, here, ho!'

"The friendly tone of our voices seemed to have changed their minds and won their confidence, for they now waited for us.

"We made signs to them that we wanted food and shelter. They understood us. They gathered sticks for us and made a fire, and gave us wherewith to eat. So we found them at last friendly, and passed the night among them, keeping a guard.

"In the morning we arose and followed the Indians to a runlet or little stream, and thence into a strange, gloomy wood where there was some underbrush that tore our armor. We showed the Indians that we wanted to find a spring of fresh water. We would fain eat our biscuit and cheese with the live water that flowed out of the earth. So we pushed on after the wandering savages.

"We came at last to a valley [Truro] full of wood-gale and long grass, and there we saw a deer at a spring, which had gone there for water.

"We hurried to the spring to drink after the deer. Oh, how clear the water ran! How refreshing it looked! We dropped down to drink. We never tasted better water than that. No ale ever was so good. It was the first time that our men drank water from the natural spring in the new land. They said that they must settle near a spring.

"We soon found other ponds [Pond Village in Truro] and came to great cornfields. Springs and cornfields, gale-fiends [bayberry] for tallow. Think of that!"

"And the Indians were friendly," said Ellen More, possibly thinking of the copper chain.

"I would have liked to have been there," said John Billington.

"You would not have left the Indians over friendly," said Pilot Coppin, "if you were up to such antics there as you are here."

The pilot continued: "We found a path. Then we came to a wonder. The path led to heaps of sand. We un-covered one of these heaps on which was a mat. We found there a mortar and a bow and arrows. The place was a grave. We had come upon an Indian graveyard.

"Then we went on over stubble fields where had been corn. Around it were great fields full of nuts, and woods still green with the matted leaves of strawberry vines.

"Listen! The path led to another wonder—to a cellar of corn, a little barn of corn, as it were, in the earth. An abandoned Indian cabin was near.

"We dug open the cellar, which was a covering of sand, and found thirty-six ears of corn. It was in a basket.

"'The corn is a treasure,' said Master Bradford, 'but it is not ours.'

"'What shall we do with it?' asked Master Hopkins.

"'Take it for our necessities,' said Standish, 'and pay for it if the owners should ever demand it.'

"The ears of corn were surrounded with shelled corn. We found a kettle there. We filled the kettle with shelled corn and bore it away on a staff. We covered up the corn bin, and agreed to tell the owners, should we ever find them, that we took the corn from necessity, and would pay them for it.

"We passed the night under the cover of a great fire. In the morning we went out again to explore, and we found another curious thing indeed. What was it?

"Listen! The queer thing that we found was a living tree bowed over almost like a hoop, so that the top touched the ground.

"'What should ever make a tree grow like that?' asked Master Hopkins, in great wonder.

"'Come here,' said one of the men. 'See here these acorns strewed around the bended top of the tree; fat ones; if I could take any more things back to the ship, I would gather them up.'

"'Don't you see,' said Stephen Hopkins, 'that tree is an Indian snare?'

"'How does it work?' asked one.

"'If you get too near it, you will find how it works. Let us away. Master Bradford,' he cried, 'come on.'

"Master Bradford was far behind us. We went on, wondering what next we would find.

"Master Bradford followed at a distance. When he came to the place of the bent tree and the acorns on the ground, he, too, was puzzled, and stopped to see what it meant.

"He went about the place here and there, when all at once we heard him cry out in a voice of great terror:

"'Ho, here, ho!'

"We looked around, and what do you think we saw? The tree had straightened up, and there was Master William Bradford tripped up and hanging by the leg.

"'Ho, here, ho!' he cried again.

"'The tree has got him,' said one of us.

"'He is caught in the Indian snare,' said Stephen Hopkins. 'Hurry back, and cut the cord. His leg may be broken. Hurry!'

"We hurried back to the place.

"'What has happened?' asked the men.

"'The tree! the tree! the tree!' he exclaimed. 'The tree has caught me!'

"'But trees do not have such cunning,' said I. 'Look here; his foot is noosed by an Indian rope.'

"'Cut the cord,' said Hopkins. 'The snare was set for a deer.'

"We cut the rope, which was curiously made. The snare was fashioned by making a noose of the rope and spreading it upon the ground under the leaves among the acorns. The tree was bent down and attached to a cross bar which would slip out of some notches when it was pulled aside, and cause the top to fly up, and the noose was tied to the top of the tree. Deer or other animals which should become entangled in the noose would cause the cross bar to fly out of the notches, and would be jerked up into the air. The Indian who set such snares visited them daily, or from time to time.

"The trapper would find the animal that had been caught alive, but sometimes with broken or dislocated limbs. A small deer would be suspended in the air.

"William Bradford did not stop to gather any acorns in that place, fat and tempting though they looked. He made the best of his time to get away, and he cast his eyes about him after that experience.

"We traveled toward the place that lay nearest to the ship. We heard whirring wings as we came. They were partridges. There were great flocks of geese and ducks in the coves. We met with a buck that had not been entrapped in a snare like William Bradford.

"The country must be a beautiful one in its season, and a goodly one to live in, except in winter, and even then it would be goodly if one had shelter, which we have not now, but will have if we remain here.

"Be happy, then. If you find a place here you will be in a land of living springs, full of health, of woods full of game, such as an English lord might covet, and of friendly

8

Indians, to whom you have only to give your hearts to find good hearts in return."

" And the copper chain! " added Ellen More.

" Hear ye all.  I have come back like the spies in the days of the wandering Hebrew tribes, and Robert Coppin has no evil report to bring of the land.  It is a land of grapes as well as of other goodly things, and no giants are there; no, no giants are there, notwithstanding the snare into which fell our good friend William Bradford! "

The Pilgrim family may have kindled the juniper fire again, and parched corn as they continued to talk over the events of that expedition.  The women's hearts were cheered.  The children's eyes glowed.

" How I wish I could get to the shore! " said sprightly John Billington.

" There are others who have the same wish for you," said one of the women, tartly.

" I would have given the Indians something if I had been there," said Ellen More, her heart always beating with generous impulses.

" Not the copper chain," said Pilot Coppin.

" No, that would have been too soon.  That is for the great chief.  I wish that *he* would come to visit us here. Pilot Coppin, could you not find him and bring him to us? Tell him that I have a copper chain for him; I would like to put it on him with my own hands."

" No, my girl; a man by the name of Hunt, a character-

_The Mayflower in Plymouth harbor._

less trader, enticed some Indians on board his ship by promises or presents, and he sailed away with them, perhaps thinking to sell them for slaves, and the Indians must remember his treachery, and they would be shy of ever going on shipboard again.

"This," he added, "is our first discovery. We are going to make another expedition, and when we return I will tell you another story, if I find anything to tell, and you may be sure that we will see some strange sights.

"I have brought some corn and acorns and red berries for the sick on board. And here are some flowers from trees that bloom in the fall. Ellen More, you may take the things to them, and speak a cheering word for me. Tell them Robert Coppin remembered them."

The little girl went to the bunks where lay the sick, with the witch-hazel blossoms, perhaps, and the presents from the land. Then the sea grew silent and the lights went out, and many dreamed of the new land of which the pilot had told them.

Little Ellen More bid Pilot Coppin good-night, saying.

"Do you think we shall ever see the great chief sitting on the green mat, and wearing the copper chain?"

"That is a fairy dream, my girl, but dream on, dream on; many fair dreams in life become things and prove true. We can not tell what awaits us."

A solitary light hung in the cabin. What would be the next story that the pilot would have to tell?

# CHAPTER XIII.

## PILOT COPPIN'S SECOND STORY.

THE shallop was being repaired on the shore.

"Let us set off on an adventure again," said Captain Jones, "and Coppin, who knows more about these parts than I do, he shall go with us."

He addressed Masters Carver and Bradford, the Pilgrim leaders.

So the women and the boys and the girls of the Mayflower saw another expedition set forth from the havened ship on the longboat, and they all waited impatiently for their pilot to return again and tell under the lonely cabin light the wonders that he saw.

Their interest in these tales of wood lore was most intense. The Pilgrims were already inclined to settle here, and the women must have favored the plan as they gazed out toward the billowy sea. Every incident that the pilot related seemed possibly associated with their future home.

He came back, and the men brought evergreens for the women and berries for the sick, and the pilot had Indian baskets which he gave to his favorites, among whom we may picture little Ellen More.

106

"Hear ye again!" he said, as the odor of the juniper filled the cabin, and the wind had a far-away sound. "Hear ye again!"

He did not lack for ears or still feet. Even John Billington was quiet for an hour. He began:

"It was a rough day when we set forth, as you know (Monday, November 27th). There were winds and cross winds, and we had to row near the shore, and when we came to land to wade in water above our knees.

"It blowed and snowed all the blind day, and then it froze. Ah-a-me, some of the people that went out will never forget that day, I mind; it made me, an old sailor, shrivel up; I can seem to feel the pitiless wind now.

"We came to a place which we called Cold Harbor [the Pamet River]. We landed, and marched through the storm up hill and down among the frozen trees that creaked as they rocked in the keen winds. Ah-a-me, ah-a-me! that was our third day out, and they were all dreadful days.

"Then we concluded to go back to the place where we had found corn, and which we well called Cornhill.

"Here we found sand heap after sand heap, little granaries or barns, or green cellars in the earth. As we laid them open the yellow corn appeared. We were obliged to break open the ground with our cutlasses, it was frozen so hard; but, rejoice everybody, we secured as much as ten bushels of corn."

"But whom did you pay for it?" asked Ellen More.

" There was no one there to pay."

" But some one worked hard to raise it; what is he to do?"

" It was probably an Indian woman," said the pilot.

" But it was as hard for her to work in the fields as for a man. What will she think when she comes back?" said Ellen.

" She will think that the needy have been to her sand barn," said the pilot.

" But why did you not leave something for her there? Some money, or some bowls, or some clothes?" asked Ellen.

" Bless your heart, my child, we hadn't anything to leave."

" You will have something next time, won't you?"

" Well, marry, marry, yes, that I will, beshrew me if I don't. I pity the Indian woman, too, when she comes back and finds her corn gone. We ought to have left some treasures for her in the baskets in the cellar. That would have shown her that we did not intend to steal, and it would have made her friendly."

" Does the winter here last long?" asked the girl.

" Yes; four months."

" Four months. Now suppose the woman who raised the corn has children, and that she comes wandering away back from somewhere for food for her children, and finds the corn gone, and nothing in her baskets to buy any?"

" Now do not worry any more about that, my little

heart. That same question is troubling Elder Brewster, as I can see. We will carry presents when we go again, to show the Indians that we mean to treat them honestly and to make them friendly." He continued his narrative:

"We sent back to the ship those who were chilled and weak, and then eighteen of us set forth on new adventures.

"On the last day of November we found beaten paths, and we resolved to follow them, which we did for five or six miles. They led us to an open field. In the middle of it was a mound, and a mat lay upon it. We knew that it was a grain bin or a grave.

"We tore up the mat.

"Under it was another mat.

"Under that was a board.

"On the board were painted the prongs of a crown.

"Here was the grave of some white wanderer. Who could have died in this lonely place?

"Then we found bowls, and trays, and dishes. I have brought back one of the dishes. Here it is. Where was it made?"

The people passed it round and turned it over.

"In France," said one of the servants, who had been on the European continent.

"We found there a bundle. It was something tied up in a blouse. It contained the bones of a man. On the head was yellow hair. No Indians have yellow hair.

" We discovered something yet more mysterious.   Hear ye all!

" It was a little bundle.

" In it were the bones of a child.   The little body was bound about with beads, white beads—here they are! "

Some of the children began to shed tears at the sight of the beads.

" The body was that of a Frenchman," said one.

" The little child was his, perhaps," said another.

" But these are Indian beads—wampum."

" The Indians buried the child," said Ellen More.   " It may have been a little girl.   I love the Indians for giving her beads—she could never reward them."

" That is so, Ellen; I thought of that.

" We left the grave, and near by we found houses made of poles bent together at the top and covered with mats.   In them were wooden bowls, trays, and dishes.   We thought that some English traders had encamped there, or had traded off these things with the Indians for corn.   There were eagles' claws there, hartshorn, parched acorns, and bundles of flags with which to make matting."   Pilot Coppin had brought back some of these things.   How strange it all seemed.

The next morning Master Carver, who acted as the Pilgrim leader, called the pilot.

" Master Coppin, can we see you in the cabin? "

" Aye, aye, at your service, sir,"

The pilot found the leaders of the Pilgrims in consultation. Should they attempt to settle here, or go out to sea again? Those who desired to settle here made these arguments, which we copy in part:

First.—There was a convenient harbor for boats, though not for ships.

Secondly.—Good corn ground ready to their hands, as they saw by experience in the goodly corn it yielded, which would again agree with the ground, and be natural seed for the same.

Thirdly.—Cape Cod was like[ly] to be a place of good fishing; for they saw daily great whales, of the best kind for oil and bone, come close aboard their ship, and, in fair weather, swim and play about it. "There was one whale," said they, "when the sun shone warm, which came and lay above water, as if it had been dead, for a good while together, within half a musket shot of the ship. At which, two were prepared to shoot, to see whether it would stir or no. He that gave fire first, his musket flew in pieces, both stock and barrel; yet, thanks be to God, neither he nor any one else was hurt with it, though many were there about. But when the whale saw its time, it gave a snuff, and away!"

Fourthly.—The place was likely to be healthful, secure, and defensible.

But the last and especial reason was, That now the heart of winter and unseasonable weather were come upon them, so that they could not go upon coasting [surveying] and discovery without danger of losing men and boat; upon which would follow the overthrow of all, especially considering what variable winds and sudden storms "do there arise." Also cold and wet lodging had so " tainted the people (for scarce any of them were free from vehement coughs) as if they should continue long in that estate it would endanger the lives of many, and breed diseases and infections among them." Again, they had yet some beer, butter, flesh, and other victuals, which would quickly be all gone; and then they should have nothing to comfort them in the great labor and toil they were like[ly] to undergo at the first.

" Others again urged greatly going to Anguum or Angoum [Agawam, now Ipswich], a place twenty leagues off to the northwards, which they had heard to be an excellent harbour for ships, [with] better ground and better fishing.

" Secondly.—For anything they knew, there might be, hard by them, a far better seat; and it should be a great hindrance to seat [settle] where we should remove again."

We take these arguments in part from the Narration of the Pilgrims. Other reasons were set forth against settling where they were.

" Robert Coppin," said the leader of the council, " you have been in these parts before, and we have heard you say that when you were here you came to a harbor beyond this, large, and opening into a fine land! "

" Yes, your honor! "

" How far was that harbor from this? "

"Some twenty-four miles, or the like of that, your honor."

"What is it called?"

"We called it Thievish Harbor, sir."

"That name has an evil sound, pilot; it bodes no good. Why did you call it that?"

"One of the Indians stole our harpoon while we were there. It is a goodly harbor, sir, and the country around it is fertile, a place of fine fishing, grand woods, and fields. It is called Patuxit by the natives. I was a sailor on the whaler Scotsman from Glasgow when I first saw it."

"Pilot, what would you advise us to do?"

"To make another expedition, sir; to see that harbor before you decide where you will settle."

They studied the maps and charts of the coast which they had brought.

"Shall we follow our pilot's advice?" said one.

The men voted to make an expedition to the harbor that the pilot had described, and so it was owing to Robert Coppin, "our pilot," that Plymouth and not Provincetown became the landing place of the Pilgrims. This counsel of the pilot in the cabin of the Mayflower is a point of history worthy of note in the celebration of the deeds of the New England pioneers. But Plymouth Harbor was not Thievish Harbor, as he dreamed. Still it was his vision of a better harbor that led to decisive events.

They had decided to make a third expedition, and the thought of it filled their minds with new plans.

" We must now consult with Coppin," said one, " and we must prepare——"

Boom!  What was that?

The ship reeled.  A scent of powder filled the cabin. Explosion followed explosion.

All started up.

" What was that? " asked all.

The women trembled.  Jasper More, who was ill, was thrown into convulsions.

A man came leading out a boy who was crying.

" Francis Billington, what have you been doing? " cried Standish in a severe voice.  " What caused that explosion? "

" Daddy's gun."

" How, you young rascal, how? "

" I took it down, and it went off."

" But there was more than one explosion, you little savage! "

" Squibs, sir."

" Who made the squibs? "

" I, sir."

" What for? "

" Because father makes 'em, sir."

" But there is a keg of powder near his bunk."

" Yes, sir."

" Where is that now? "

"It is there, sir."

"Run!" cried several voices.

The women screamed.

The boldest men ran to the Billington bunk.

The musket was there, the exploded squibs, with weapons and pieces of iron. But the keg, or rather half a keg, of powder stood there harmless. Had a single spark reached it the history of the Mayflower and of the Pilgrim company would probably then and there have come to an end.

# CHAPTER XIV.

THE Billingtons, we are led to suppose, were a rather unquiet family, though perhaps to this restlessness may be due the early discovery of the so-called Billington Sea. John Billington, Sr., came to a terrible end, as we have said, and whether his wife's tongue was as sharp as has been represented we do not know, but one of her boys, as we have seen, came near blowing up the Mayflower in his strange experiments with his father's powder, and another John Billington threw the colony into great excitement in the first summer after the landing, as we shall relate in our narrative.

"Raree show," said John Bilington one day, with the shores in sight. "Raree show!"

"And what do you mean by that?" asked Pilot Coppin.

"Wouldn't it be a jolly thing to go hunting for Indians, and take them back to England and show them for a wonder? Then one could bring them back as pilots, and discover gold mines and the places where the old arrow makers hid their treasures. Raree show!"

"Raree show!" cried Francis Billington, whose fancy

116

was awakened by the suggestion of Indians on exhibition in London.

"That would not happen," said Pilot Coppin; "if you were to go hunting Indians you would not capture them, they would capture you! 'Raree show! Raree show!' They would put you up on exhibition in the owl swamp, and the owls would call out 'Whoo? whoo?' That would make a 'raree show' for the ravens to caw at, and the woods are black with crows!"

"My folks are always agitating something or other," said Mistress Billington. "What my boys will come to goes beyond my ken. If they do not capture Indians, the Indians will be likely to capture them. John's head is always in the wrong place, and the hands of Francis are usually found in the same quarter."

"Shall we see Tusquantum should we land here?" asked Ellen More. "You told us how he was kidnaped and carried away."

"It is not unlikely that we may find him."

"He could talk for us with the other Indians," said Ellen More. "He understands English."

"The trumpets of the winds are sounding again," said Wrastle Brewster. "Pilot Coppin, the ship is at anchor, and you have nothing to do. Tell us other stories of the Indians of whom you have heard—stories of adventures in these parts, told by returned sailors on the English docks."

"Tell us more stories about kidnaped Indians," said

young John Billington, " for my mind already goes roaming
through the forests, and I will one day meet with adventures
there."

" And I," said his brother Francis.

" You have already had adventures enough to satisfy a
fleet," said Mistress Billington. " Where would we have
been had a spark touched that keg of powder? And fire all
around that keg, and squibs bursting! Oh, it drives me
wild when I think of it! "

" Kidnaping," said Pilot Coppin, " is an evil business.
When Pinzon, one of Columbus's captains, stole four Indians to sell them for slaves, Columbus commanded that
they be set free, and in that he showed his nobility of character. Kidnapers are usually kidnaped in some form in the
end, for the law of justice must be fulfilled, and to every
man be meted the measure wherewith he metes."

He continued: " John Verazzini, the Florentine in the
service of Francis I, had some strange experiences among
the savages, we are told. Sailing along the New England
coast in 1524, nearly a hundred years ago, he landed some
twenty men, who went into the interior. When the Indians beheld the white men in armor they took to their
heels, probably thinking that they were gods or monsters.

" But there was one old woman who could not hobble
away. Old as she was, she carried a child on her back,
in the Indian way, and there was a young woman with her,
about eighteen years of age, who had three children on her

back. The old woman was filled with the greatest terror when she saw the white men coming, and the young woman, burdened with the children, was greatly terrified. The braves ran; they had neither old age nor children on their backs to hinder them.

"There was a meadow of bright grass near. The old woman suddenly sank down in the grass, and lay perfectly still. The young woman did the same, and the grass waved like a sea, and had not these poor people been seen to disappear there, the meadows would only have seemed to be inhabited by the Indian birds, which they call conquiddles.

"But the sailors dashed into the grass after them.

"When the old woman saw that she was discovered, she set up a wild howling, and the children followed her example. The young woman sprang up, and it was a quick wit she had.

"She pointed to the way the men had gone, and cried out in Indian: 'Gone! gone! there! there! go! go!'

"I do not blame her for sending these strange men after her people, since they had deserted her with her babies.

"They attempted to seize and carry her away, but she kept up such a noise as made them willing to let her go. They kidnaped one of her children and took it away. Verrazzini, on another voyage, was himself captured by Indians, and it is said that he was eaten by them."

He continued: "Some nine years ago Captain Edward Harlow was sent out to discover the island of Cape Cod.

9

He sailed past this place, and found that Cape Cod was not an island at all, but a part of the mainland. He enticed three Indians whom he met on Montregon Island to come on board his ship. One of these Indians was called Pechmo.

"When Pechmo found that the English intended to make him a captive he leaped overboard and escaped.

"The ship's boat hung over the stern. One day Captain Harlow was astonished to find that the other two savages were gone, and that the boat had disappeared. Pechmo had returned under the cover of the night or a storm, cut the boat from under the stern, and helped his comrades to escape.

"'We must rescue the boat,' said Harlow.

"He cast his eyes on the shore.

"'There it is,' said he. 'Bring it back!'

"They set out in some light craft to bring it back. When the sailors came to where the boat lay they found it filled with sand.

"'We must clean it out,' said the mate.

"They were about to do so when a shower of arrows fell among them. The boat, filled with sand, had been moored under the cover of bushes or trees, or some safe protection. The men were glad to get safely back again.

"Now, many such things had happened on the coast, and the Indians must have come to believe that the traders are thieves."

"Ellen!"

It was the voice of Mistress Carver.

"Jasper is going to leave us. The voyage has been too hard for your little brother. He is dying."

The Mores were four orphan children. They had been taken into the families of the Pilgrims in Holland: Ellen into the family of Edward Winslow, Jasper More into that of John Carver, and the others into that of Elder William Brewster. It seems strange that these Pilgrim families should have brought the orphans with them. Only one of these children lived to grow up, and he changed his name to Mann.

Ellen More followed Mistress Carver to the bunk where her brother was lying, faded and white.

He looked up to Ellen.

The wind was whistling in the rigging, and the boy must have known that his grave would soon be made in the sea.

"I pity you, brother," said Ellen More. "What can I do?"

"Is the pilot on board?"

The girl turned swiftly away.

"Pilot Coppin, come. I can do nothing. Oh, do come! Jasper is going away. What can you do?—do something—quick!"

The pilot came and stood above the dying boy.

"Pilot?"

"Well, my boy?"

"You have been good to Ellen."

He lay very still. The broad form of Elder Brewster bent above the four little orphans.

"Pilot," whispered the boy, "I am going to father and mother now. It would make me happy to kiss your hand."

The pilot put his hard hand to the white lips, but the power to move those little lips was forever gone.

The little form lay still and white.

They wrapped it up. The pilot took it into his arms and went away and left it by itself, and when he came back his arms were empty, but he bent down and kissed Ellen More.

Did he take it with him that day as he went on board the shallop? It was hard weather that day, and the ocean would make no account that another little form had been added to its unnumbered graves.

When Ellen asked about her brother's remains she was told that they had been taken away by our pilot.

"What our Pilot does is well," said Elder Brewster.

"Our Pilot"—she understood in part all the good man would imply. Yes, heart of little Ellen More; yes, heart of the great ocean of the multitudinous waves, what our Pilot does is well, in all the providential mysteries of the world.

Those were hard, dark days; if we have sprinkled a little fiction for the sake of illustration in our vision of the past, the narrative is substantially true. Those were days of child heroes on the sea, and their little hearts, like the souls of the Pilgrim mothers, shared the common suffering. But the harvest of all good endeavor and good work is sure, and they who seek their happiness in spiritual things, and live for the welfare of all men and all time, will not in the end be disappointed. This little colony, for whom waited not so much as a roof, a fireplace, or any comfort in the cold, was to give expression to ideas which would furnish the model of a great republic that should dominate mankind. So right ideas grow and triumph in the world.

# CHAPTER XV.

THE third expedition of discovery, this one under Pilot Coppin, sailed away from the Mayflower on December 6th. Those who remained on board eagerly awaited the return of the explorers.

It was Sunday on the Mayflower, December 10 (20th).

The tide had gone out of the harbor, leaving the channels lying like open rivers, and had come back again, over those dark meadows of the sea. The fourteen men who had gone out under "our pilot" in search of a place of good anchorage, a land of springs of fresh water and of broad timber, had not come back again. They were on Clarke's Island then, as the place is called to-day, and was named so then for the first time.

The people were gathering, many of them helpless and weak, in the cabin to receive words of comfort from Elder William Brewster, one of the most beautiful characters to be found in the records of mankind. The young people gathered there, and they came with willing ears, for they had come to regard this great-hearted, loving man as a father.

124

All gathered in a circle. There were two dogs on board, and they too came, and Mistress Billington was about to say "Scat!" to them, when we may see good Elder Brewster passing by and saying: "Let the dumb creatures listen, so that they be quiet."

The ship rocked to and fro. It was probably the first meeting house and pulpit in the empty New England world.

The people sat with folded arms. It was the darkest day in all their lives, and they wondered what the glorious man of faith, verging on sixty, would say.

We can not know now what his words were, but their meaning may come to us in sympathetic interpretation.

"Since we last met two of our number have been laid away in the sea and many have sickened, and fourteen have gone out from us into the stress of the cloud and storm to seek for a place of habitation. He who knows the end from the beginning has guided us well.

"My hair is turning gray, and I stand before you as your servant, having no will but to serve you. I have given up all my worldly possessions for this service, as you all know. I have sought no worldly gain or honor. I stand before you as your elder, conscious of my needs, and only waiting for that blessed man, John Robinson, to come over the sea.

"I do not often speak of myself, as you also know, and if I so speak to-day it is but to show you that I seek nothing here but to be your servant in faith, and to carry the Gospel to those tribes who have never heard the word.

"My manner of life to this day is known to you all. I was a student of Cambridge, and I served the court under that goodly gentleman, William Davidson, for eleven years. I was sent with him by the queen into the Low Countries, in Leicester's time, and the keys of Flushing were given to me to keep. After such affairs of state I returned to my father's house at Scrooby, and there united with that church and society that has crossed the stormy sea. I have been imprisoned for the good of this people; I have turned my back on honors and public gifts for the sake of this people; I have given up my private fortune for you, and, bless God, I stand before you to-day, on this rocking ship, with empty hands. I am simply your elder, and I would never seek to be your pastor, lest you should say of me that I sought for myself what belongs only to the elect ministry of God.

"But was there ever on earth a company of God like this? The sea rocks beneath, the sky lowers above us, and the winds whistle around us, but we have Faith. We are driven as exiles into a wilderness of savages, but we have Faith that the cross of redemption arose even for them. We know not whence our food is to come, but we have Faith; whence our shelter is to come, but we have Faith. The plague of the sea is upon us, but we have Faith. We may perish after the view of men, but we have Faith. There is a Faith that overcomes the world, and a Faith that is over-

come by the world, and living is dying; we have the Faith
that overcomes the world."

Little Ellen More was there.   She had put on her neck
the copper chain.

When the good elder had gone to all the bunks to speak
out of his good heart of faith to the sick, he touched the little
girl on the shoulder.

"Why do you wear the gift chain, my little one?"

"Not for ornament, sir."

"I knew that; your little heart could have no vanity
like that in these dark days."

"I put it on, sir, because I have Faith."

"That gives my heart help, my little one.   Faith in what,
may I ask?"

"Faith that I am carrying the chain to the forest king,
and that that king will wear it in love and protect us all.
Pilot Coppin thinks God's gift of love to the great king is
in this chain."

"Pilot Coppin is a good man.   There are not many like
him.   He practices well what I try to preach.

"Little one, did you know that I once received a gold
chain to wear?" he continued.   "It was a Holland chain."

"No, no, was it?   Where is it now?" asked Ellen
eagerly.

"It was only given me to wear in honor of the states.
It belonged to the secretary of the queen, and I gave it back
to him.   Your chain minds me of it."

"You gave back your gold chain, and I am to give up mine? You wore your chain that the queen might be pleased that you had served her, did you not?"

"Yes, yes, that the queen might see that the Netherlands had approved of what I had tried to do."

"I am wearing my chain for a king."

"What king?"

"The Indian king. Pilot Coppin will tell you about him."

"What faith! You are the Syrophœnecian woman's real little daughter."

"That is a long word, Elder Brewster; who was she?"

"Ask Elizabeth Winslow, your foster mother, some other time, when you are alone with her. She will tell you her story."

A disease like the scurvy was threatening the people on board, and especially the women and the servants. The one desire of all hearts was to reach land, to feel again the steady earth under their feet.

"If we must perish, let us die on the land," said one woman to another.

"I am so weary, so weary," said Rose Standish, "but I will never complain; I hold to the faith of Brewster, who counts all gains as losses for the sake of the cause of the Cross in the world."

"Oh, that they would come back," said Elizabeth Winslow, "and tell us that they had found a place of springs!"

Elder Brewster heard, and answered:

" ' All my springs are in thee.' "

Night came, and the ship rocked and rocked even in the haven, in which a thousand ships might find shelter. The lamp light swung, the sickness increased. Even the two dogs caught the depression of that dreariest of all the dreary nights on the Mayflower, and howled.

Yet to-morrow would be a day that would cause the merry bells of the world to ring for these tempest-tossed people, and that for a thousand years. But they could know nothing of this, save by faith.

The statue of Faith rises over Plymouth Harbor, with its face toward the serene blue sky. It stands for more than any other statue in the Western world, and when the traveler sits down beneath it and looks up to it, his eyes fill with tears, and he chokes to speak, and he knows the meaning of the apostolic words, " of whom the world was not worthy." He himself must be destitute of worth whose heart does not melt there, and feel the aspiration for a better life.

Such was the life on the Mayflower during those perilous days, of which Pilot Coppin will give an account to those who are waiting his return.

Let us continue the picture. How did the Pilgrims who were left on board the Mayflower during the expedition feel as they watched for the return of the explorers on the winter coast? The leading men of the company were among the explorers, except Elder Brewster and John Alden.

# CHAPTER XVI.

## THE ROCK OF FAITH.

It was December 12th (22d).

"They are coming," cried the Billington boys, who were ever on the alert.

"Scat!" said Mistress Helen Billington to the dogs, which seemed to have scented land, and started up at every announcement that caused an excitement on board.

"What do you suppose that they have found?"

It was a blue day, and the boat of the explorers rose clearly in view.

Elder Brewster looked off on the harbor, and John Alden, the cooper, stood beside him. In popular tradition John Alden disputes with Mary Chilton the honor of being the first to step on Plymouth Rock. John Alden did not go out with the explorers at all. At the final landing of the Pilgrim company at a later date, he or Mary Chilton, as we shall picture, may have been the first to stand upon the rock. A long legend gives the honor to Mary Chilton, who married John Winslow, Governor Edward Winslow's brother, whose tomb may be seen from Tremont Street in King's Chapel burying ground, Boston. The famous Com-

*Plymouth Rock.*

mander Winslow, of the Grand Pré romance, was of this family.

The boat came on, the people crowding to the rail of the ship to welcome it. John Howland, who had been washed overboard during the voyage and marvelously rescued, and who is supposed to have sung amid the storm that beat upon the explorers, is seen to turn his hearty face toward the ship.

"Oh! he! ho! Good harbor!" shouted he.

"Good harbor!" echoed the company.

"Springs!"

"Springs!" echoed all.

"Timber!"

"Timber!" chorused the company.

"The clouds are lifting," said Elder Brewster. "The Old World lies behind us—the gates of the New World are opening. I can see them as in a vision. The hand of Love is behind all events."

"Good cheer! good cheer!" rang out a voice. Whether John Howland really sang in the storm or not, Robert Coppin did cry out, "Good cheer!" when he saw Plymouth Harbor, and we may well suppose that he cried "Good cheer!" now.

He merits the name of Good Cheer Coppin from this time. It may be said that Plymouth Harbor was not the one of his dreams. But he was certainly the pilot that directed the Pilgrims to Plymouth Harbor, though he came

near carrying them north, and who must have thrilled
the hearts of the men when he first saw the harbor by the
cry of "Good cheer! Good cheer!" an exclamation
worthy to give a name to some Plymouth school or insti-
tution.

"Good cheer!" answered all to the heart of Pilot Coppin. Even the dogs barked in the general joy.

Up the side of the ship climb the explorers. The sails
go up again; the anchor is lifted. The Mayflower moves
on again in clearer air toward Plymouth Harbor, and enters
the deep channels of the wide haven, so beautiful in calm, so
dreary in storm. Good Cheer Coppin, what story hast thou
now to tell?

They stood on the deck again—the men who had found
the rock and the springs: Robert Coppin, pilot, the leader;
Governor Carver, William Bradford, Edward Winslow,
John Tilley and Edward Tilley, two inseparable brothers;
Richmond Warren and Edward Doty, and John Clarke, the
mate of the Mayflower, and several sailors.

The people pressed around them.

"It is no common story that I bring you now," began
Pilot Coppin, on his return, as he sat down amid the company, as before; "there are few accounts that can surpass
it, I mind. If you shall found a colony, and it shall grow,
what will the people of the future say of the song that was
sung when the sky lashed the billows, and darkness filled
the sea, when the rudder hung loose, and the sails were torn,

and men lay sick and dying? They will say that Faith has
not failed in the world.

"Listen again, and I will tell you what we saw.

"From the beginning the wind was cold, and the blasts
beat upon us. The spray dashed over us and froze on our
clothes, and we were clad in coats of ice that were heavy
as iron.

"Edward Tilley fell back as one dead, and his brother
watched over him. Our gunner was also sick unto death.

"Out into the heavy waters we sailed; we saw a point
ahead at last where we might come to shore. Indians were
there and a fire. We spent the night on the shore, and then
divided into two companies, one to go on by water and
one by land. We came together again at night and encamped, setting a sentinel. We prayed there in the light of
the fire, and then we sang a psalm. Oh, to have heard those
men singing in the woods by the sea in the storm! That
was a song of Faith.

"The fire blazed warm against the black night. Then
we lay down, and all was still save the dashing of the sea.

"Suddenly at midnight the sentinel cried:

"'Arm! arm!'

"We rose up. There was a hideous cry in the air. We
discharged two muskets; then all became still again, and we
concluded that it was wild beasts or sea monsters that we
had heard.

"In the morning we knelt upon the ground and prayed

for guidance and protection. Then we carried our arms down to a place near where the shallop lay and laid them down on the ground.

" A cry rent the air. It was wild and strange and hostile. It was like the cry that we had heard at midnight.

" One of the company who had gone into the woods came running back, crying 'Indians! Indians!'

" There was a rattling in the trees. It was a shower of arrows.

" 'Collect your arms!' said Standish. He had kept his own snaphance [a hand gun fired by a flint and steel]. We hurried to recover our arms.

"The cry of the Indians was now loud, wild, and fearful. It was like this: 'Woath! Woath! Ha! Ha! Woath!'

" The trees, as it were, became Indians, and the Indians trees. The trees with big trunks seemed to encase Indians. We could see plumed heads peer around the bark of such trees and disappear.

" We discharged our pieces, but we might as well have fired into the empty air.

" At last one of the Indians was wounded, and he uttered a dismal cry—so woeful that it went to the hearts of the rest. He fled, and all followed his example. They probably did not understand our death-dealing pieces.

" It was a dark morning. We went out from our shelter and found eighteen arrows on the ground. Here is one of them; it is headed with a hart's horn. The encounter took place at Neuset [Eastham].

"We started out upon the sea again, hoping for good weather, but it began to snow and rain. The wind rose in the afternoon and the seas rolled rough; the stays of the rudder broke and two men made a rudder of their oars.

"In this terrible water I yet felt a light within. It was Faith.

"'Good cheer, be of good cheer, all!' I cried. But we had but Faith to give us good cheer. Outside of that light everything seemed to be going against us.

"There came a fearful blast, and the sea tossed and our mast split in pieces.

"'Good cheer, be of good cheer, all!' I cried again. 'I can see the harbor!' Then Master Howland sang. Was there ever a song like that? *

"I gave a wrong command, but that was overruled by the hand of an unknown power. We fell upon an island.

"Our mate, Clarke, was the first to leap to the shore.

"'I seize the land in the name of King James!' he cried. So we called the place Clarke's Island.

"We built our fires in the darkness, prayed, and sang again. The next day we rested there, for it was the Sabbath. We found a great rock there where we assembled, and in the afternoon and sunset of that still day we saw the

---

* It seems to have been a tradition that this man sang amid the storm.

10

great harbor lying in the distance to which Providence had directed my soul.

"We could sing the psalms of Leyden in these perilous days. Winslow, Bradford, and Hopkins could pray and give counsel, and John Howland sang—the man servant of our governor—may his life be long! *

"Monday morning broke clear; the dark sea rolled calmer and the blue sky arched the subsiding waves.

" 'That is not your harbor,' said the men to me.

" 'No,' I answered, 'that is not the harbor that I saw on the Scotsman from Glasgow, but it is your harbor, and the one to which Providence has directed you.'

"We got ready to sail into that harbor, and entered it on more quiet water.

" 'There is a great rock yonder,' said John Howland, the singer, 'let us land there.'

"The rock stood out in the shallow water like a monument. We drifted up to it. John Howland leaped upon it in the name of King James of England. We are going to lift anchor and go back there, the place to which I directed them, though that was not the harbor that I had then in my mind.

"The harbor is marked on the chart by the name of New Plymouth, after the beloved Plymouth, where the people

---

* Mrs. Hemans has made use of this tradition:

"Amid the storm they sung,
And the stars heard, and the sea."

*The canopy under which Plymouth Rock is now preserved.*

were kind to us in our distress. It is not Thievish Harbor, as I supposed; you will be glad of that. It is a place of springs, of living waters, pure and cool.

" On that strange rock—whence did it come?—you, too, may land. It looks as though Heaven set it there as a lonely wharf to signal the souls of heroes. Happy is the woman who shall first set her foot upon it. If Providence is indeed your guide, her name shall live in a glory more great than Captain Miles Standish ever won in Flanders."

So the pilot's dream of a better harbor had ended well. His invisible faith would one day turn into a monument.

We have no love for those who try to destroy great national traditions. Nearly all such legends are found, after all, to rest on a firm basis of fact. But the traditions that Mary Chilton or John Alden were the first of the Pilgrims to step upon Plymouth Rock, as we have shown, can not be true. No woman accompanied the Pilgrims on the expedition led by Pilot Coppin in the open boat, and John Alden, as we have related, was not with them. The tradition in regard to Mary Chilton is likely to be true in the general landing of the Pilgrim company, when the women and children left the ship, but that event did not occur on Forefathers' Day. What matters it? In substance the forefather legend is true.

The Faith of that day no one can ever dispute, and the victory was in the Faith, as achievement always is. To the eleventh chapter of Hebrews we may add: " By faith America was discovered by Columbus and in faith the Pilgrim Fathers founded the nation." It is unwritten Scripture, but it is as true as that in the famous chapter which has been called the Westminster Abbey of Hebrew History.

# CHAPTER XVII.

THE Mayflower is on the sea again. She is headed for the rock, for the land of the living springs. From one of these springs, at the place of the old Bradford house, the visitor to Plymouth yet may drink. It is a public fountain now.

The young folks talked of what they would do when they had landed, and Mistress Brewster sat down beside her boys, who bore the curious names of Love and Wrastle, the last, we suppose, in reference to the story of Jacob and the angel. Mary Allerton joined the company—she who outlived all the Pilgrims, dying in 1699, having lived at Plymouth nearly eighty years.

"What can a boy do in a country like that?" said Love Brewster.

"Build," said Joseph Rogers. "It is builders that live. What they build is their thoughts and life. If I live I will build, and I will begin to build by helping others to build."

"That is a proper and sensible thing for a boy to say," said Mistress Brewster. "Now, John Billington, I have some fears about you. What will you do? Something useful, I hope."

"I'll become an Indian chief; that would be the most useful thing anybody can do."

"And I'll help him," piped Francis Billington.

"Beshrew the boy!" profanely said Helen Billington, or "Goody Billington," his mother. "Hear him now— if he'd a-gone only a little further with his squibs we'd all have been drowned. An Indian chief—Mistress Brewster, the trouble is that my boys' minds are too active. I think that they will make discoveries."

"I would like to discover Tusquanto, or Tusquantum, about whom the pilot told."

"And why Tusquantum?" asked Mistress Billington.

"Why, Goody mother, he would be a tongue for us. He lived with Sir Ferdinando Gorges for years, and was educated by the trader. He would be a tongue for us."

"We will need a tongue, an Indian tongue," said Mistress Brewster. "Now that was a sensible remark. You can be sensible. I do think that the boy who could find Tusquantum would be very useful to us. Now good thoughts are the souls of good actions. May be that you may find Tusquantum. Who knows?"

"Let us look over the presents again," said Love Brewster.

"Yes, yes, bring out the box of presents that we are going to give to the friendly Indians—to those who do us service," said Mistress Brewster.  "It makes the heart mellow to look over the things that we expect to give away."

Love Brewster brought a curious box.  Many of the people had followed the counsel of Pilot Coppin, who had advised the Pilgrims to purchase gifts in Leyden to be offered to the Indians, and had brought gifts with them, beside the copper chain.

"Now, gifts are heart money," said Mistress Brewster, "and here is our treasury.  Here are knives—I wonder who will receive them—and scissors—I hope some of the Indian women will receive those.  And here are necklaces—the Indians are very fond of necklaces, the pilot says."

"Here is a tin whistle," said Mistress Billington. "That's yours, John.  You'd better keep it yourself; you may need it when you get lost in the woods, going to be an Indian chief."

"Mary," said Mistress Brewster to Mary Allerton, "let us have a little treat now.  You are a careful girl.  You may go to my chest and bring out the looking-glass, and we'll all look into it and see how we look in this strange country before we land.  Handle it very carefully.  John Robinson himself may have looked into that glass.  It would be a goodly sight if all the faces that have been seen in that glass could appear on it again."

Elder Brewster's looking-glass, the supposed looking-glass of our narrative, is still to be seen at the old Brewster house in Plympton near Plymouth.  All of the Pilgrims, and probably John Robinson, may have seen their faces in that glass. What a revelation, indeed, it would be could it bring back again all of the faces that had passed before it!

The looking-glass was brought out by the careful hands of Mary Allerton, perhaps out of the traditional chest, yet to be seen, whose hinges turned the leaf of a new destiny in the world.

"We have looked into it before," said Mistress Brewster. "We will now look into it for the last time together. Whatever the Pilgrim men may do in making a colony, there will never much be known of the Pilgrim women, I think. But whether we live or perish, we have been faithful and true."

She passed the glass from one to another carefully. The whole company gathered in a little circle to see how they looked before they set foot upon the land. It was like the opening of a family album to-day, only the faces vanished with the look, and the glass could never bring them back again.

What faces looked into the glass, and wondered what would be their destiny in this new world of storms and waves!

Some of the women wept when they saw how their faces had grown thin and faded.

"Never mind," said Mary Allerton, "summer will come, and that will bring us everything—so the pilot says!"

The faces lightened.

" Here, Rose Standish, you may see now," said Mistress
Brewster, passing the glass.

Rose Standish had dreamed of finding Virginia, a land
of fair skies, sunshine, and flowers, and not this land of
snows. She saw how thin and white she had grown as she
looked into the glass. But there was Faith in her face.
Miles Standish, one of the heroes of Flanders, had not sailed
on any vain purpose for the new land, however rugged the
shores might be found.

" Miles is a brave man," she said, " and I must be a
brave woman. Faith is everything, but I have faded some."

New faces crowded around Mistress Brewster to look
into the wonderful glass, which to them was like a magic
mirror. Mistress Catharine Carver was there, and Mistress
Elizabeth Winslow, both of them soon to die on the white
shores of the land now lying in view.

Mistress Martin was there, the wife of the treasurer of
the company, who also would fall a victim to the hard life
in the winter woods.

Susanna White was there, the mother of the first white
child born in New England.

Mistresses Hopkins, Tilley, Tinker, Ridgedale, Chilton,
Fuller, and Eaton were there, and these all were to fall before the sickness that would come upon the colony.

Lively Mary Chilton looked into the glass, and Priscilla
Mullins peeped shyly over her shoulder.

" And now let me and my two rapscallions have a look,"

said Mistress Billington, who, like her family, was noted for her almost profane manner of speaking.

"Scat!" she said to her son John; "let your mother look first. Well, I do look as though I couldn't help it—I do declare! don't I now? Now, John, 'tis your turn; you don't look much like an Indian chief now; you'd better not let any Indian chief get hold of you. And don't you ever go to wandering anywhere into the woods; 'tis a very uncertain mind that you have. We may have to give away some of these knives and curious things to ransom you from some savage. The Indians will be more likely to get you than you will be to find some ancient arrow maker and to become a chief. Scat!"

This last exclamation was addressed to John, after the pseudo young chief had taken a peep into the magic glass.

"Now let your brother look—he that is going to help you find Tusquantum and to become a chief. They say that the great king of the woods here has a brother chief. There—scat!"

She pushed Francis, of the powder episode, away from the glass, and said in a kindly tone, "Now let the children have a look. If we are going to have any future in these empty woods—how the wind howls!—it is to be in them. Here, children, come and look, and I'll be a mother to you. I have a good heart, now, if I do talk rough."

Ellen More looked into the glass. Mistress Billington was about to say "Scat!" but she saw tears in Ellen's eyes, and she drew the girl to her bosom and said, "You poor little motherless child!"

"Never mind, Goody Billington," said Ellen, "never mind; the pilot will come back again!"

"What makes you think so much of him, Ellen?"

"Oh, he thinks good things."

"That he does—now, he does. He talks by what he does, now—Pilot Coppin don't boast of being a good man, but he *is* a good man, and I love him, my girl, because he loves you.

"Scat! scat! scat!"

What had happened now?

The Billington boys were breathing upon the precious glass, and drawing their fingers over the mist.

"Always in some mischief! What made you think of that? Your heads are loose! There, go!"

The rough, kindly woman gave them a push.

"Here, Mary," said Mistress Brewster, "you may put the looking-glass away again, very carefully, very carefully. We may never *all* look into it again."

On, on moved the Mayflower. The sky was black and billowy, and the waves seemed lashing each other. The white wings of sea birds rose through the cold mist and spray. The ship came to anchor.

In several of the bunks were sick people. It was dark by day and darker by night, and there were no sun, moon, or stars.

Yet the founders of a nation were rocking on those wild waves. The cabin light burned as it hung and swung, but it was the light of Faith in all these hearts that was to be the torch of destiny.

Would they ever find the great forest lord with the simple offering of the copper chain? Would they ever meet Tusquantum and make him their tongue to the Indian tribes? And would the summer that was thought to bring them all things ever come, with warmth and healing, flowers and birds, and memories that would make them doubly grateful for the blooming fields and winged skies? We shall see. Faith beckons them on.

They are in quiet waters now. Pilot Coppin points out to the wathful eyes the famous rock.

"Good cheer!" he said. "Behind the rock are springs, and behind the springs rise the hills where we may build. Good cheer!"

"Good cheer! good cheer!" echoed the voices of the women and children.

A party of men landed to hew timber and to prepare for the landing of the Pilgrim company, which was soon to follow.

"We are going on shore," said Pilot Coppin to young John Billington; "what can I do for you when I get there?"

"Find Tusquantum, and I will find the way to all good fortune, sir!"

" Aye, aye! you are keen, my boy—it is an Indian to speak for us that we will need to find if we are to live in peace with the natives.  And now, Ellen, my little girl of the Mayflower, what can I do for you?"

" Find the great chieftain of all the lands, and tell him we have brought for him a copper chain from the lands of his brother kings over the sea!"

" Aye, aye, my girl of the Mayflower, I will look for them both—Tusquantum and Massasoit, or Ousamequin, as some call him."

" That will be a great day, Pilot Coppin."

" Yes, my little one, a great day."

" And *he* will sit under the great trees?"

" The great trees with beards of moss!"

" Smoking a pipe of peace?"

" Yes; the forest king, not the trees."

" And will he wear a plume?"

" Aye, aye, he will be all paint and shells and feathers."

" And great lords will be around him?"

" Aye, aye, the lords of the forest, with bows and quivers."

" They will not shoot their arms?"

" No, no; they will stand up straight like images.  They will not shoot.  Their wampum belts will shine in the sun."

" What is wampum, Pilot Coppin?"

" Shells—shells of pearl."

" Will the women be there? "

" Likely—they have girdles of shells."

" And plumes? "

" Yes, the plumes of the eagle, or the purple jay that bobs his head when he spies you, and says ' Haw, haw!' "

" Oh, I am so glad, Master Coppin! You will not let John go off and be a chief, will you? He's nothing but a boy."

" It would be a sorry day if John should ever find himself among the Indians. They would take him to make sport for them, I fear."

" You will see what I will do when we land," said John. They did.

How the children of the Mayflower must have looked out upon that desolate shore! How they must have contrasted it with Leyden, and Delft, and Southampton, and old Plymouth! Instead of ivied walls and towers and ringing bells, a single rock. Instead of gay shops, a promise of a few frozen springs. Instead of homes, woods of which to build houses.

" Each family must build its own house, and all must erect a Common House," said the governor. In this plan was begun the New England village.

The company was now prepared to land. Pilot Coppin gently bore down to the ship's boat the light form of little Ellen More.

The pilot helped the women carefully, remembering

Mrs. Bradford, who had been drowned from the Mayflower. So the women and children set foot on the rock in the homeless land.

At this landing of a rather uncertain date, we may repeat that Mary Chilton (Winslow) may have been the first of the Pilgrims to set foot on Plymouth Rock. She probably was, else there would not have been such a tradition among the descendants of the Pilgrims. The explorers landed on December 11th (21), and the Pilgrim company at a little later date, and so it is true that December 21st is Forefathers' Day, now usually celebrated on the 22d.

The Pilgrim company could hardly have landed at any one time, for there was serious sickness on board. The Mayflower lay off in the harbor that Pilot Coppin had hailed with "Good cheer!" and the shallop and longboat passed to and fro between the ship and the land.

Good Cheer Coppin's work is not over. The Mayflower is to lie here until the birds come back again in the blue skies of an early spring. The Pilgrims are yet to face a terrible winter on land, but the genial New England spring is to come in early March, and when Pilot Coppin shall say "Good cheer! spring has come again!" the colony will have begun that long era of glorious life in the current of which we find ourselves now, in that grand stream of the ocean of human destiny. We must follow these events.

And now the Pilgrim Fathers are upon the land. They pass Christmas Day in felling trees, and the captain of the

Mayflower entertains them on board in the evening.  He probably told them tales of the Halloweens or the Christmas greens of their old home of the hollies and ivies; or perhaps causes John Howland to sing of the mistletoes.  We know not.  Captain Jones was a rough, jolly man, and we do not like to believe that he betrayed the Pilgrims and brought them here by stealth.  He was true to them in the winter of their sorrows.

They must build a Common House, a place for public worship, a fort, and must bring to the fort their cannon, and for all these things the Mayflower must wait.  They must make some seven houses for the heads of the families; these they must fashion of timber cut from the trees, and cover with thatch.  The trees are there, monarchs of the forests. The meadows of thatch are there, glistening with ice foam by the sea.  Hack, hack, hack, sound the axes.  The thatch gatherers are at work in the keen gray mornings.  The sick still wait on board the ship.  It is in this way that the new nation begins to build.

But the reaction from the voyage comes, a kind of scurvy, a fever of exhaustion, and many sicken and die. The serving men die, Rose Standish dies, several of the children die.  The hardship of the sea seems to follow them.

But the work of the building goes on.  The sickness increases.  The winter is wild, snowy, and cold.  Wolves howl in the forest.  But February lights up the earth, and the bluebirds come out of the woods.  The mornings grow red, and the angels of spring are in the air. Spring came early that year in the true sense of the term. March was like April.

The green mat was rolled up in the Common House, and the copper chain was still a thing of faith—it was waiting.

Who can picture the distress of that winter? One after another dying in the Common House!

They must bury the dead at night, lest the Indians should know their helpless condition; they must dig the graves deep, lest the wolves should uncover them.

When some were burning with fever, the deep storms came, the sea winds driving the bulletlike snow against the rude walls of the house made of logs and clay. The wind drifted in, drove the smoke down the chimney, and often made the company hover together for warmth.

They went o ꞏ very still in the night with the bodies of the dead. They waited for the moon to rise to bury the wasted forms in the rude coffins. The carpenters must have spent their nights in the solemn work of preparing boxes for the dead.

Imagine a scene on such a night! The moon rises on the white, silent snows, and hangs over the cold, glittering harbor. Afar in the dark forests, where the pine boughs are covered with ice, wolves—called "lions"—are howling for food. The sky is red in the distance with an Indian camp fire.

Out of the Common House come the bearers in the keen

11

air with the body of the dead. They bear the burden on their backs to the hill. The gravedigger, with his dark lantern, meets them there. They lower the body into the deep earth. They hear the wolves howl. No words are spoken. The grave is filled in the moonlight, is leveled and covered with snow. Night after night, with short intervals, the silent scene is repeated. The moon has not often looked down on a spectacle more pitiable.

The lights of Leyden were three thousands miles away. The native inhabitants of the land were dead except a few wandering families. Even the wild cat knew not where to find its prey, so dead and empty was the land, and so pitiless were the cold and storms.

In that awful January and February what would a historian have written in his book of prophecy? Ye who sit by your warm fires in luxurious rooms may well recall the days of old New England, for in those terrible times the faith of the Pilgrim Fathers never failed or faltered. There was " no room in the inn," but the magi were on the march, and the star of destiny hung in the clouds over those eight or more rude houses by the sea.

# CHAPTER XVIII.

## IN THE WOODS.

THE first thing that the Pilgrims did on landing from the ship, now moored in Plymouth Harbor, was to build a Common House. This was to serve as a shelter for all, for a place of public worship. The country was already named New Plymouth on the old chart, and report has it that it was named by Prince Charles. The first house was named the Common House. It would serve for a fort, or a place of defense, until a stronger fortification could be built. The place of the Common House is still marked in Plymouth. It is near the rock.

To this house the sick were to be brought. Here the goods of the ship were to be stored for a time. Here for the first days of their history on shore the Pilgrims lived as one family. Here almost daily the people sickened and some died.

John Billington and his sons, whom we are sorry to record from Morton as "one of the profanest families amongst them," were at once restless and eager to explore.

"Captain's mate," said the senior Billington one day, "let us make a journey into the woods and see what we can find. Let us make a journey of discovery. Everything seems very silent here. There must be something to be found. I climbed a tree the other day, and thought I saw a sea."

"May I go, father?" said young John Billington.

"Why should you want to go, John?"

"To find the ancient arrow maker," said John.

"No, not now. There are always ancient 'arrow makers' in your head, and I wonder if such imaginations will ever bring you any good."

The two men set out, carrying but a single musket.

"We may be in danger," said the mate. "We have seen fires in the woods not many miles away ever since we landed."

"Yes, and we may not be in danger. The Standish party found nothing alarming when they went out to explore, and they brought home an eagle. It was a beautiful bird, and they roasted it and they say that it tasted as sweet as the meat of a lamb. I did not get a taste of it."

"One bird could not be divided among a hundred hungry people," said the mate.

The woods hung with withered grapes and glowed with bitter red berries. Partridges flew up from the red and yellow seed pods of leafless rose bushes. There were rabbit tracks here and there, and green patches of teaberries and princes' pine.

Strawberry leaves carpeted the open places, covered with frost, but retaining their summer color. It was Roger Williams who said that God might have made a better berry than the strawberry, but he did not, and the same Pilgrim found strawberries so abundant that " a ship could have been loaded with them."

Suddenly the mate cried " Halt! "

John Billington stopped. Before them rose some deserted houses made of poles.

" Indians," said the mate.

" There are none there now—there is no smoke."

" Let us move cautiously," said the mate. " We may be struck with arrows."

" The arrows are not poisonous," said Billington. " Those were not that we found in the first encounter."

The two men approached the huts with sharp eyes. There was no movement within.

There was water near. It was a sea. It grew as they went on.

In the midst of the sea was an island. It was a beautiful spot in the primeval forest. It may be seen to-day as it was of old, a few miles out of Plymouth, and it is still called " Billington's Sea."

If there were Indians there they hid themselves. The Indians felt that they had good reason to hide from the white adventurers, even when they were superior in numbers, for a number of them had been stolen from Cape Cod, and the two or three who had returned must have told very alarming stories of England and Spain, as Pilot Coppin's stories have already revealed.

They returned to the Common House, where William Bradford fell sick, and to which the news was brought that Christopher Martin, the treasurer, was dying on board the Mayflower.

"Have you brought home nothing, father?" asked young John Billington.

"Nothing—there was nothing to bring."

"What did you find, father?"

"A sea and an island. I could not bring them back with me. They will stay where they are."

"They can do us no good. Did you see any Indians there?"

"No, but we saw the place where they lived. That would be a good place for you to go and be chief; a no Indian chief of no Indians. It is a fine country."

"Did you find it?" asked Mistress Helen.

"What, Mistress Helen?"

"The discovery that you were to make."

"I found a sea!"

"A sea? What good did it do for you to climb up a tree and discover nothing? Clarke found an island and Coppin a harbor, and all you have discovered was a sea. You did not even bring home an eagle. Scat! scat! Land of mercy! what was that?"

A little chipmunk ran out of one of the logs, and darted under the blockhouse.

"That was not a mouse or a rat," said she. "It was striped. He's gone for good; he was a squirrel like. What a good soup he would make," she added, with sudden good-heartedness, "for some of the sick people here! There are more and more falling sick, and I pity them. What did we ever leave London for?"

It would be hard to say, but the family left to the sea a name, and that sea came to be associated with a sad history.

# CHAPTER XIX.

THE sickness increased. A hospital was built and a storehouse. Lots were assigned to heads of families, and houses, made of oak and clay, and roofed with thatch, were built for the Pilgrims who had families.

We have spoken of dogs on the ship. The company brought with them two dogs to Plymouth, one of these a huge mastiff, which seems to have been called Hero, and belonged to John Goodman. The other was a spaniel, and is assigned to Peter Browne, who died at Plymouth, 1633.

As thatch was of great service in roofing houses, the cutting of thatch in the abundant sea meadows became a very useful employment. The thatch was best cut at low tide, was bound in bundles, and left to dry upon the shore.

Among the thatch gatherers were the same John Goodman and Peter Browne. John Goodman may have lost his life by thatch gathering, we can not be sure, but he did not long survive a most terrible adventure.

Four men had gone out to cut and bind thatch, and of these were John Goodman and Peter Browne, who took the

158

mastiff and spaniel with them.    Noon came to them after
some hours of labor, and John Goodman and Browne being
friends went away together to eat their meal.    They came
upon a pond of fresh water, and hastening toward it saw
there a deer.

"Isn't it beautiful?" said Goodman.    "A stag—look
at its antlers!"

The dogs saw the stag and crept around their masters,
waiting for a signal to give chase to the animal.

"Let the dogs give chase," said Browne.    "We've
sickles to dispatch it if they bring it down.    Hero, hist
—go!"

The great mastiff started, the spaniel following.    The
stag looked up for a moment, lifting its head high in the air,
then bounded away.

The dogs and stag were soon lost to view, but the men
followed the cry of the dogs.    The chase became exciting,
and the two men heeded not whither they were going.    On,
on, went the animals, and on the men, following the cry in
the empty woods and through thickets, until suddenly the
dogs became silent.

"What has happened now?" said Browne, panting.

"The dogs have lost the stag," said Goodman.

It was so.    In a short time the dogs came back to them
panting, and crouched down as though ashamed of their
failure.    How the stag escaped the men could not know.
It may have leaped some stream.

" Where are we?" said Goodman.

" Which way is east? There is no sun."

" The dogs must lead us," said Browne. " Here, Hero, home!"

But the dog, which understood the word and knew what to do in its own land, could not obey the direction here. It followed the scent of animals, rather than the course back again.

The shadows of the afternoon were falling. The men wandered around and around, following the bewildered dogs, and night came on, and the woods were black and starless.

" We must get to the shelter of some thick trees and remain there until morning," said Goodman.

" But it is bitter cold," said Browne, " and our clothing is poor. We shall perish before morning. See, snow is falling, only it is too cold to snow hard."

The cold increased. It became terrible.

" We must walk around and around the tree all night long," said Goodman. " We should die were we to go to sleep. My feet are like ice. I must keep the blood circulating. Walk! walk!"

" It is easy to say that, but my feet are numb. Where will the people think that we are gone?"

" They will think that we have been captured by the Indians, and we shall add to their trouble in the sickness. Why did we lose our senses? Walk! walk!"

Around and around a clump of high trees they ran. But the night grew more and more severe.

A cry echoed through the forest.

"What was that?" asked Browne.

"A lion [wolf]. Walk! walk!"

"We must climb the trees. Is there no way to make a fire?"

"None—walk! walk!"

The mastiff began to answer the wolf with a cry of defiance and seemed about to break away from them.

Browne seized the dog, saying:

"I must hold it. We must not let it go away from us—we may need it here."

Another cry rang through the black forest, and another.

"There are a pack of them near," said Goodman. "But we mustn't climb the trees till they are upon us, and we must set the dogs on them should they come."

The dogs howled, barked, and cried savagely. The wolves were unused to such sounds and seemed to fear them. They barked, but kept at bay.

The excitement of the situation roused the latent blood of the men. They walked violently, and stopped to listen. They caught each other in their arms, and struggled with each other to keep their blood warm. But with all their efforts Browne cried: "My feet are frozen; I fear that I shall never see the ship again."

" Walk! walk! " still cried Goodman, and the two kept on going round and round in the dark circle.

Morning came at last. Goodman dragged Browne to the foot of a hill, and leaving him there went to the top and climbed a tree.

" Cheer up! " he cried. " Browne, Browne, up, up, come on! "

" What do you see? " called Browne.

" The harbor."

" What else? I am numb."

" I see the ship."

" Come down to me, I can not walk more."

" I see smoke. Fire—fire—where there is smoke there is fire. Keep up heart. I am coming down! "

He came down, but Browne was unable to move farther.

He clasped him under the arms and dragged him forward, Hero following and howling.

Goodman put his life into the struggle. He loved his friend and would die rather than leave him.

" Home! " said the half-frozen man to Hero.

The dog could follow human tracks now and obeyed.

The people heard the dog call and ran out of the Common House. They took the poor thatch gatherer in their arms and bore him home.

" We thought that the Indians had carried you away," said distracted Helen Billington.

" Scat! " she cried out to the faithful dog. " Take the

cripple to Dr. Fuller in the new house. The governor is there!"

They carried him to the new house. Governor Carver received him there and laid him down before the fire.

Dr. Fuller tried to take off the poor man's shoes. They were frozen to his feet.

"Shall I live, doctor?" faltered Browne.

"Yes, yes, you will live."

"But Goodman, will he live?"

"He is not frozen," said the doctor.

"No, no," said Goodman. "My being compelled to carry him is what saved me."

He turned white.

"Goodman, Goodman, this is not the end. I may live, but it will be through your life. I do not care for myself, but I do care for you—I love you as my own life."

"I have no children. You have. I'm all right, all right."

The doctor grasped his hand and felt of his pulse.

"You are coming round again," said he.

Browne did come round again. He recovered from his affliction slowly, but was for a long time lame.

But Goodman had received a shock, and for him there was small hope of recovery. His strength had gone out of him.

"If it must be one of us, it had better be I," we may

fancy him to have said, for such seems to have been his spirit.

He hobbled about for a time. One day his spaniel was attacked by two wolves and ran for protection between its master's legs. Goodman secured a stake and threw it at the wolves, which, we are told, sat down and "grinned at him."

The poor spaniel was not used to such company as this.

Goodman seems never to have been well after that dark night in the woods. One night he died.

They had heard a cry of Indians about New Plymouth the night before. They must not know that men were dying; they must not know that there were graves on the hill.

So they went out at night and broke the frozen sod, and they carried the body to the hill and laid it into the earth. They covered it with the clods of earth, and covered the clods of earth with snow, and the next snowstorm covered all.

The hill lay white in the morning, and the spaniel howled for its good master at night, but John Goodman would never share his meal with the beautiful animal again.

# CHAPTER XX.

To John Billington and his wife Helen was assigned the charge of the Common House. Their sons, John and Francis, were not the most trustworthy boys to live in such a place, but John seems to have desired to see Indians, and if the latter were to appear anywhere in town it would be there.

Robert Coppin came over from the ship from time to time to talk with the young people, and the old, as well, in the Common House.

Indians were lurking around. Great columns of smoke rose here and there in the distance like pillars of the sky. The heavens were red at night with camp fires, or forest fires where camps had been. One day two Indians appeared on a hill beckoning.

John Billington, the boy, saw them and came running home screaming, setting his nervous mother in a tremor. Miles Standish and John Hopkins went out to meet the Indians, and the latter disappeared.

" And you never asked them to make you their chief," said Pilot Coppin to John in a bantering way. " What did they look like? "

"I didn't look long," said the boy. "One of them said 'Hoach,' and that word did sound awful. When you find Tusquantum I will ask him what it means."

"'Ah he' means yes in Indian," said Coppin, "and 'keen' is art thou. 'Pinese' or 'pnise' means one who talks with the dead."

"If I had said to one of them 'Keen pnise?' he would have said 'Ah he'?"

"He might have so answered; perhaps he was not a prophet."

"He didn't look like a prophet—the one that waved his hand around *so*, and *so*, and *so*," said John.

Helen Billington looked upon the boy with staring eyes.

"He will keep venturing," said she, "farther and farther, and some day he'll meet an Indian that will whirl him around *so*, and *so*, and *so!*"

Ellen More sat in terror before the Common House fire as she listened to this startling prophecy.

"They are mounting the cannon," said she. "They say the minion weighs twelve thousand pounds, and the sacre fifteen hundred pounds, and they have made Miles Standish captain. I hope the captain will never fire those guns upon the Indians. I wish that he would send for the great chief to come here. The chief could lay down his arms on the other side of the brook, couldn't he?"

"Yes, yes, my simple-hearted little girl, that he could."

"Then we could give him the copper chain and the

jewel, and make a feast for him, and ask him to come again and bring his wife and children."

"His wife and children! His squaw," said Mistress Billington, "and his papooses."

"What is a squaw? That don't sound well."

"The squaw-sachem, she means," said Pilot Coppin. "The queen."

"That sounds well. What was that other word, Mistress Billington?"

"His papooses, you poor little simpleton."

"What's papooses, Mistress Billington?"

"His little naked brats," said the woman, who is supposed not to have been overnice in descriptive words.

"He wouldn't do that, would he?"

"Why, child, the chief is a great big, black, half-naked savage; a giant, painted like a painted image, such as you used to see in the museum of Leyden. And he grins—just like that!" Helen Billington made a dreadful grimace.

"O Mistress Billington! I'm sorry for him if he acts like that. Now I think the copper chain would look real pretty on him. It would make him lift up his eyebrows *so*, and look pleasant."

"He will make ye lift up your eyebrows *so*, and look pleasant if he were to get his hand into your hair. He tomahawks 'em!"

"O Mistress Billington! that sounds *sad*. What is that?"

12

Robert Coppin put up his hand.

"The little girl need not be told about such things until she gets older. Let her keep her illusions of the great forest chief sitting under the oaks wearing the copper chain."

"She might as well fancy a bear with a crown on his head eating out of a silver tureen with a gold spoon. But let the girl dream her dreams. She looks peaked. I hope that she is not going in the way that her little brother went."

"I think that I will live to see the chief sitting under the trees, with the birds all singing around him, and see him lift up his eyebrows so, real friendly and pleasant like. Elder Brewster says that everything is possible to faith."

"That's right, my own little girl. Let us have faith. I have faith; one thing what we came here for was that our faith might be free."

Ellen More lived in the new house of Edward Winslow, the traveler, and Mistress Winslow's goodness of heart is seen in making a home for this little orphan girl.

There were a few pleasant days, sky blue days, in that short and terrible winter. On such days Pilot Coppin would come over from the Mayflower when there was nothing for him to do, and help the Pilgrims in their building. He could use the jackscrew in the mounting of guns.

"It has saved us once," we may fancy him to say, "and it shall now be used to protect the company it saved."

"Ay, ay," said the ship's carpenter, "that was a lucky thought that brought the jackscrew on board and saved the main beams. Success is the product of tools; the more things we provide for ourselves to help us the more we advance. 'Tis the things that lift that help life."

" Yes," said Pilot Coppin, " and it is those people who lift and not lean that make good colonists. We can not know how much that jackscrew has done for the world, or rather the thought that caused the jackscrew to lift the main beam, and that won the battle of the ship against the seas."

On one of the sky blue days Pilot Coppin said to Mistress Winslow: " The voyage has told upon you. You need sunshine. Let us go out on the beach and gather shells. We will take, if you like, Ellen with us."

" O Pilot Coppin! you have the good cheer for us all that was in your heart when you saw the harbor. I am not well; the sunny air may give me new life; let us go."

They went down to the shore, the pilot leading Ellen by the hand.

It was low tide. The sea seemed almost to have left the harbor, except in the deep channels which looked like rivers. Great blackfish lay about, looking like rocks. The floor of the harbor was covered with shells. In the far sea whales were spouting.

There was kelp everywhere, and at places there were piles of shells that the Indians had thrown away in their transient settlements.

Ellen picked up a very curious shell on the beach, among the dead starfish.

" What a queer shell that is, Pilot Coppin!  I never saw one so beautiful."

" That is a pettywinkle," said the pilot, picking another mollusk of the same kind out of some kelp in which it had become entangled.  " Some call it the periwinkle.  Is yours dead? "

" I do not know—how can I tell? "

" Put it up to your ear and listen."

Pilot Coppin handed his shell to Mistress Winslow.

The good woman and Ellen both put the shells to their ears.

" What do you hear? " asked Pilot Coppin.

" I hear, I hear the sea; I hear, I hear England, and the murmur of winds and bees amid the hedge rows; I hear, I hear the voices of my soul! "

Mistress Winslow held the shell to her ear as she spoke.

" What do you hear, Ellen? "

" I hear, I hear the far away—the far, far away.  What makes it do so? "

" The echo of the ocean is in it," said Pilot Coppin.  " The dead shell sings forever of the ocean."

" It makes one feel that life is an ocean," said Mistress Winslow; " that the soul is on an ocean of which we know not the beginning nor the end.  I am going to take my shell back home.  I will listen to it when I am lonely.  How that sound does make me feel—so lonely, so little, and yet

*The fort and meeting-house, 1671.*

so full of hope! It gives me faith where everything is vast; all must be well."

Ellen found a larger periwinkle, and took both of the shells home with her.

" Will they sing of the sea by the fire?" asked Ellen.

" Yes, they will sing of the sea by the fire or anywhere, and they will forever sing of the sea. They seem to say that this world may be small, but that life is large, and better things await us far away!"

" I feel that is true, Pilot Coppin, and whether we live or die we are all pilots like you, and may I be like you, a pilot of good cheer, whatever may happen. I sometimes think that I shall not live long."

Ellen More stood dumb at these words, and her lips quivered.

" I think of Jasper," she said, " when I listen to the shell. What good did my little brother's life do, Master Coppin?"

" He made better the hearts of those who cared for him, and those who loved him, and who remember him."

" It may be that I will make you happier for loving me, Pilot Coppin."

" That you have already. The ocean has a million waves every minute, and it could not do without one of them. We all need each other, and the Pilgrims need the children; it was the children that caused them to sail in the far away world of which the shell sings."

Elizabeth Winslow tottered as she entered the new house under the thatched roof.

She put the shell on the rough log shelf over the fire-place.

The people came in and were told of the song in the shell. They heard it and wondered. They, too, went out and gathered periwinkles and ornamented the rude shelves of their cabins with them. The first ornaments of the house were probably the periwinkle shells. Such shells have been favorite adornments of the Pilgrim homes, and may still be found on the beaches and in the old houses. They sing of a larger life than any other music, of a larger world for the soul and of infinite hope.

The memory of the periwinkle deserves to be cherished, like the arbutus flower, among the things that awaken Pilgrim memories. No music better interprets the thought of these prisoners of hope in their thatched cabins on these shores by the stormy winter sea.

# CHAPTER XXI.

THE INDIAN MILL.—A CURIOUS EVENT.

JOHN BILLINGTON, Senior, often went out to explore, and his sons followed his example.

One day they came home bearing some corn husks. Pilot Coppin was at the Common House when they came in, and at once took a lively interest in what they had found.

" The land of Goshen! " said Mistress Billington, " what have you brought home now? Husks? Where did you find so many? "

" Near the mill, mother," said John Billington.

" What is that? "

" A rock with a hollow and a great stone pestle, like that for a mortar. The Indians have been grinding or pounding corn there. They threw away the husks, and I have brought home some of them."

" What will you do with them? "

" Strip them and make a pillow of them," said John.

" We could braid them and make mats of them," said Mistress Billington. " They would braid like strips of cloth. What kind of a place was it where you found them? "

"There were tulip trees there, and withered trilliam, and bayberries, and red berries."

"One might make tallow out of the bayberry," then said our pilot. "The land must be full of things that we can learn to use. Even the walnuts would yield us oil. I will go with you, John Billington, some day to see the Indian mill."

One day in February Pilot Coppin and the two Billington boys set out for the mill. It was found near a cornfield, and great heaps of husks were near. The ground squirrels had taken possession of these, and darted away under cover when they saw strangers approaching. The corn was ground here by breaking it with a stone pestle and rolling over it a huge round stone as it lay in the hollow of the rock. The Indian women did the grinding.

There were gardens here where beans had grown. The favorite Indian dish in that country was succotash, made of corn and beans boiled with venison. This also became a common food among the Pilgrims.

All was silent in the place except the notes of the pilfering blue jays.

The three sat down on the grinding rock. Suddenly one of the great husk heaps stirred, and presently it toppled over and a head rose out of it. The apparition seemed to be an Indian woman.

She threw up her arms with a sound like "warregah"; she kept her form out of sight under the husks and writhed about with terror; she probably had never seen a white man before.

She began to scatter the heap about in such a way that the flying husks filled the air.  Higher and higher they flew, then the cloud settled down in a heap again, but there was no woman to be seen.

"She has been playing partridge," said Pilot Coppin. " Hark! "

Far away through the green tangle of brier bushes by the side of the cornfields, there arose a wild cry of terror. " Warregah! "

"She is calling to some one," said Pilot Coppin.

They carried back husks from the deserted mill, and John Billington told the story of the partridge trick in the Common House.

" Ah, never did that happen except in your mind, boy; there are no Indians about here now, or only wanderers," said Mistress Billington.  " You see them in your mind; some folks see ghosts that have guilt on their consciences."

But a thatch gatherer soon after saw twelve Indians near the town, and hid in the thatch while they passed, and Miles Standish lost his tools in the wood about the same time.  Some one had carried them away, and it could not have been any of the colony.  Now and then, here and there, signs of Indians lurking about the settlement were to be seen.  Were these Indians friendly or hostile? "

At night the far heavens glowed, as they had done for a

long time, from Indian fires. The settlement wore an air of mystery at such times, as the moon rose golden, like a night sun over the sea.

There were sweet teaberries or checkerberries, partridge berries, and chestnuts in burs, to be found in the woods. These made the evening in the Common House cheerful at times, especially when the winds blew, the snow flew, and lions (wolves) were heard in the deep woods afar.

John Alden was the youngest of the men. He was a cooper. After the death of Rose Standish he became intimate with Miles Standish, and the two found much in common in the principle of supply and want which is a law of brotherly friendships.

One morning when the advent of spring was in the air, Mistress Billington chanced to open the door of the Common House; as she did so she threw back her hands and cried:

" Scat! "

She stepped back, then renewed her courage, and exclaimed:

" What are you standing there for? Go home and put on your clothes. Did I ever see the like? Nothing but an apron on this cold day. Scat! "

The men in the room started up. A giant stood in the door. He wore only a girdle and apron for decency; his head was plumed, and by his side was a bow and two arrows.

The men came to the door. John Alden was there and Miles Standish. The men had gathered there to consult

about an expedition, they having made Miles Standish the
captain of their forces.

The Indian's face lighted with a friendly expression as he
said:

" WELCOME, ENGLISHMEN! "

The men were filled with wonder, and while they were
at a loss as to what to say, the lusty visitor exclaimed:

" I am Samoset—a chief."

" Whence did you come? "

" From where the wind comes in full moon—from the
north."

" How can you speak English? " asked John Alden.

" I have lived among the traders on the North [Maine]
coast!   I talk English a little; Tusquantum speaks English better; he has lived in the Englishman's country."

John Billington, the lad, came leaping to the door.

" Do you know Tusquantum? " he cried.   " Let me
signal for Pilot Coppin."

The news of the arrival of Samoset ran through the
place.   John Alden brought a gay shawl or blanket and
put it over the Indian's shoulders that he might appear more
presentable to the women, and thus quieted the indigna-
tion of Mistress Billington.

Edward Winslow came hurrying toward the Common
House, followed by Elder Brewster.   Ellen More came to
the door and looked in, and seeing the chief or sagamore
sitting within as in a robe of state, she exclaimed:

"John Billington, let us go to the hill and signal."

"I have signaled, Ellen."

The men, led by Governor Carver, gave Samoset a warm greeting. They set before him hot drinks and meat, and built a great fire.

At noon Pilot Coppin came from the ship, and in the afternoon all the men sat down to talk with Samoset.

He told them tales of the chiefs and sagamores, and pictured the glory of Massasoit, whose kingdom extended from the capes to the bays.

"He once went forth in mighty power," he said of Massasoit, "attended by thousands of warriors. When he stamped his feet the Narragansetts trembled and the Pequots hid. Then the great Death came—the dark spirit that swept away the warriors. The braves died in heaps; they turned yellow; there were none to bury them. Their bones lie white in the empty forests, and the wind whistles among them when it bends the trees. Only one is left; he went away from the place because he saw the spirits of the dead when he wandered alone. The dead warriors came back again!"

In the midst of his narration Captain Miles Standish strode to and fro.

"Samoset," he said at last, "they have made me a captain here—a sagamore. I am to do justice here for the governor. Your people have been lurking in hiding about the place. That is not right. Some of them have stolen

my axes and wedges, and have carried them away. That
is not right. They must bring the tools back again, or I
shall lay them on the earth with my firearm. Standish has
to speak so; justice compels him to speak so; Standish has
spoken."

The new captain stamped his foot on the split log floor.
The master of the Common House rolled the big drum.

" Thunder," said Samoset.

" You must summon your people to bring back the
tools." The drum rolled again. Samoset may have
thought that the master of the Common House was the same
that rolled the " thunder drum " of the spies. Be that as it
may, he was cowed and overawed by the big little captain,
and he evidently determined to recover the lost tools.

They sheltered him that night at the house of Stephen
Hopkins, and set a guard over the place.

" Welcome, Englishmen! " the words passed from lip
to lip.

" Samoset," said Pilot Coppin, " I have told the people
here of Tusquantum. Do you know Tusquantum? "

" Samoset knows Tusquantum. He meets him in the
hunting grounds. Tusquantum is the only Indian left
alive in Pawtuxet. He has lived in the Englishman's
country."

" Samoset must bring Tusquantum here."

" Samoset will seek him out and bring him here. The
ghosts will not follow him now. He is afraid that the Eng-

lish will carry him away again in their big canoes.    But
you do right.    Your captain puts his foot down *so!*"

Little Ellen More wanted to speak to this forest lord.

"May I?" she asked of Pilot Coppin.

"Yes, yes, speak!" said the pilot.

"I wish I might see Massasoit," said she.

"He is a very big man for a little one to see—he is a
mighty chief."

Little Ellen shrunk away, but she still kept the hope that
she would one day bear to him, mighty as he was, the copper chain.

When Samoset went away the Pilgrims presented him
with a knife, a bracelet, and a ring.

He returned in a few days bringing other Indians with
him.

The party were decently and picturesquely dressed, and
painted and plumed.

They left their weapons on the ground before approaching the place.

Samoset came in proudly.    He carried a bundle in his
hands.    He saluted Miles Standish respectfully, and laid
down the bundle at his feet.

He opened the parcel.    In it were the missing tools.

Such an example of honor should have won the hearts
of the Pilgrims.    It should have shown them the possibili-
ties of the Indian character.    Pilot Coppin's heart responded
to such a truly noble deed.

" It is a good tale that I will have to tell of you, Samoset, on the docks of London or Southampton. The people will here bear me witness that I have always spoken well of your race. I wish I could relate what I have seen to-day to King James himself, but that a poor pilot like me will never be called to do. But men who carry good reports do good in the world. I can do that."

" Pilot, you speak of King James. How does King James look? Is he as grand to look upon as the great Massasoit? "

" I have never seen the great Massasoit, Samoset. I want to see him before I sail away. I wish to carry over the sea to the traders good reports of him."

" He is larger than your captain, pilot. I wish to ask you one thing more: Does King James do justice to his people, as Massasoit does? Would he have returned the lost tools? Those tools were not stolen—they were found."

" Governor Carver, you must answer me here. Does King James always do justice in his dealings with men? Heaven forbid that I should judge the king. Elder Brewster, you should reply for me."

Elder Brewster must have thought of English prisons and persecutions and confiscations as he saw the restored tools lying upon the ground. But could he say that the pagan king was more honest than his own?

" Ask me not now! Melchizedek paid tribute to Abra-

ham. It may be like that now. I wish to see the great
Massasoit."

Samoset lifted his hands.

"HE IS COMING! He is on his way; the great Massasoit
is coming!"

Ellen More clapped her hands as she heard this announcement. She hurried back to Mistress Elizabeth Winslow.

"Massasoit is coming—the great Massasoit is coming!"
she cried.

"We must lay the green rug for him," said the lady,
who had been used to ceremony.

"He has sent back the lost tools to the captain," said
Ellen. "The captain spoke hard to Samoset when he asked
him to find the tools. You do not think that Massasoit is a
better man than the captain, do you?"

"He is a pagan," said Mistress Winslow. "But any
king who puts honor above self-interest deserves to be entertained upon a field of cloth of gold. Massasoit shall have
my green rug when he comes—it is the most beautiful of
the goods of the colony. I believe him to be every inch a
king!"

Mistress Winslow brought out the rug and spread it out
on the floor. Ellen laid the copper chain upon it.

"Thoughts are things sometimes," said Mistress Winslow.

"I dreamed of it," said Ellen. "I shall see it, and the

spring is coming—the bluebirds are here already, and the pilot says that they bring the spring on their wings.   Oh, I am so glad! "

She danced about saying, " Massasoit is coming! "   Had the king been an old friend of hers she could not have been more happy.

# CHAPTER XXII.

## MASSASOIT.—THE COPPER CHAIN.

THERE is one coming to New Plymouth who is truly noble—not noble because he is hoping to gain something, or fearing to lose something, not noble because he has schemes by which he would bring other men into slavery, but noble because it is noble to be noble, and because to have a royal nature is a debt that a king owes to his place among men. He did right because it was right; we wonder if King James himself, who claimed to own the country because English explorers had discovered it, was really as noble as this grand forest king, who spake to the Pilgrim Fathers the truth in benevolence, and who kept his word for forty years, and that after the descendants of the Pilgrims had broken the sacred promises of the Fathers.

It was Thursday, March 22, 1621, " a fair, warm day."

In the flood of light under the blue sky the forest birds were singing. The pink arbutus, full of odor, was breaking through the melting snows; the forest streams were running down the slopes, where the maples were turning red.

Plumes rose above the line of what is now called Watson's Hill, a height overlooking the town.

*View of Leyden Street, Plymouth colony.*

"They are coming!" shouted the young people around the Common House.

The people rushed out of their houses to a point where they could see the advancing plumes.

Massasoit was indeed coming with his brother Prince Quadequina, who always attended him.  This brotherly affection of Massasoit, who was also called Ousamequin, for his brother was one of the characteristics of the king which it is pleasing to recall and record.

The king and the prince had with them sixty warriors, men of great stature.  They were plumed and painted, and armed with bows made of the springing woods of the forest.

They stopped on the brow of the hill and looked down on the Pilgrim settlement and upon the harbor where the Mayflower lay.

First to the Pilgrims came Samoset again.  He had brought with him another Indian, who had not the air of a dweller in the forest.

"I am Tusquantum," said the latter, addressing Governor Carver.  "I have seen the land of the white king, and have lived in his country.  Tusquantum is a friend of the Englishman.  I am come to say that Massasoit is coming to visit you.  He is now here."

There was in the company one who we may fancy hoped to find in Tusquantum a teacher; it was John Billington.  It is said that John Billington, Senior, had been a poacher in England; be that as it may, he had an adventurous spirit, and his sons inherited the same.

"The tongue of the English has come," said Pilot Coppin, who had made known the value of such a man as Tusquantum, or Squanto, as he came to be called by the English.

So came Squanto before the royal train appeared.

The royal Indians now beckoned from the hill. It was not thought wise to send Governor Carver to the king, though an act of confidence would have been most worthy.

The Indian king, some of whose subjects had been treacherously stolen and carried away to be sold as slaves, could not be certain that he would not be betrayed by the new settlers. So he would not come down the hill until he had first made an understanding with the Pilgrims.

"I will go to the king," said Edward Winslow. Mistress Winslow unrolled again the green mat, and Ellen More brought out the copper chain for the ceremony of the welcoming of the chief.

"Here are a pair of knives as a present to the king," said Carver.

"And here are the copper chain and jewel," said Ellen More.

The little girl felt that she had somehow fulfilled a mission in the world.

Edward Winslow advanced to the hill beneath which ran a brook. He wore an armor and carried a sword. In his pockets were presents, and on his arm was the copper chain.

The scene is so pleasantly described in Morton's, or Mourt's, Narration, that we give it here. Here is Mourt's record of it:

"Thursday, the 22d of March [1621], was a very warm day.

"About noon, we met again about our public business; but we had scarce been an hour together, but Samoset came again; and Squanto, the only [surviving] native of Patuxet, where we now inhabit (who was one of the twenty captives that, by Hunt, were carried away; and had been in England, and dwelt in Cornhill [London] with Master John Slaney, a Merchant; and could speak a little English), with three others; and they brought with them some few skins to truck; and some red herrings newly taken and dried, but not salted.

"And [they] signified unto us, that their great Sagamore Masasoyt was hard by, with Quadequina his brother, and all their men. They could not well express in English what they would; but, after an hour, the King came to the top of a hill over against us [Watson's Hill], and had in his train sixty men; that we could well behold them, and they us.

"We were not willing to send our Governor [John Carver] to them; and they [were] unwilling to come to us. So Squanto went again unto him, who brought word that we should send one to parley with him; which we did, which was Edward Winslow; to know his mind, and to signify the mind and will of our Governor, which was to have trading and peace with him.

" We send to the King a pair of knives, and a copper chain with a jewel to it.  To Quadequina, we send likewise a knife, and a jewel to hang in his ear.   And withal a pot of strong water [spirits, brandy?]; a good quantity of biscuit and some butter, which were all willingly accepted."

Edward Winslow approached the king and the prince on the hill.

" I salute you, O king, in the name of your brother over the sea, King James of England, France and Ireland.

" My king salutes you with words of love, O Massasoit.

" My king sends through us his messages of peace, O Massasoit.

" I am come to be a hostage, O king.   I will remain here while you shall go down and cross the brook, and meet my king's people there.   The governor there awaits you."

" I would not keep you, O messenger, as an hostage," said Massasoit.   " There need be no such thing among men of honor and faith.  Let us go down to the brook and meet the messengers of your king, the white brother from over the sea! "

" I will remain here with Quadequina," said Edward Winslow; " but before you go, I wish to present to you in the name of our king, your white brother, and for the governor here, and all his people, and the men on yon ship lying on the sea, this chain and jewel. It stands, O king, for friendship, for love, for peace, for brotherhood. May I put it upon your neck? "

Massasoit took the copper chain. As he held it up the jewel twinkled in the sun, and the light of it made the heart of little Ellen More dance on that bright March day. Her dream was fulfilled.

Then Massasoit with a stately tread, wearing the copper chain, came slowly down the hill toward the brook.

Captain Miles Standish with a half dozen musketeers advanced to meet him.

As the king came to the edge of the sunny, rippling water, the six musketeers fired their muskets.

The sound of so many muskets astonished Massasoit. He saw that the English had secret power.

They brought the green rug from the house of Edward Winslow, and laid it down for Massasoit. He sat down upon it.

Little Ellen More had gone to Pilot Coppin, and had taken him by the hand.

" See, see," she said, " he is wearing the copper chain. It will be well with us here. Do you think he looks as noble as King James? "

Here is the account of the event from Mourt's Narration or Journal:

" Captain Standish and Master Allerton met the King at

the brook with a half dozen volunteers.  They saluted him,
and he them.  So on going over, the one on the one side, and
the other on the other, conducted him to a house, then building, where we placed a green rug and three or four cush-
ions."

As soon as Massassoit was seated on the green rug a
trumpet sounded, and a drum rolled through the air.

Governor John Carver with more musketeers was coming down from the Common House to meet the king.

The governor bowed low as Massasoit arose and extended his hand.  Governor Carver took the red hand and
kissed it.  Then the two conferred together, and a banquet
was prepared for them.

In that conference they made a treaty of peace.

It was a treaty that, simple as it is, is worthy of immortal
record.  The primer of the brotherhood of man is in it.
The heart of the Indian king flowed forth in the goodness
that seeks the universal good of mankind.

Read it, analyze it, this treaty of the copper chain, with
so many lying dead on Burial Hill, with so many hearts
beating with hope and faith, and the Mayflower lying in the
harbor:

" 1. That neither he, nor any of his, should injure, or
do hurt, to any of our people.

" 2. And if any of his did hurt any of ours, he should
send the offender [to us] that we might punish him.

" 3. That if any of our tools were taken away, when our

people were at work, he should cause them to be restored; and if ours did any harm to any of his, we should do the like to them.

"4. If any did unjustly war against him, we would aid him. If any did war against us, he should aid us.

"5. He should send to his neighbor[ing] confederates, to certify them of this, that they might not wrong us; but might be likewise comprised in the Conditions of Peace.

"6. That when their men came to us, they should leave their bows and arrows behind them, as we should do our pieces, when we came to them.

"7. Lastly, that doing this, King James would esteem him as his friend and ally.

"All of which the King seemed to like well; and it was applauded of his followers," says Mourt, and adds:

"All the while he sat by the Governor, he trembled for fear."

How did Massasoit look? The old recorder says:

"In person, he is a very lusty man, in his best years, [of] an able body, grave of countenance, and spare of speech. In his attire, [he was] little or nothing differing from the rest of his followers; only in a great chain of white bone beads about his neck; and at it, behind his neck, hangs a little bag of tobacco, which he drank [smoked] and gave us to drink [smoke]."

The treaty that was then concluded lasted forty years,

and the pledge that accompanied it is one of the most poetic
events of our history.

What was the pledge?

It was made in the gift of the copper chain.

"While you shall wear this chain, the red man and the
white man shall live in peace," in effect said the Pilgrim
legislation.

"Massasoit will never cease to wear the chain," said the
king, or like words. "Whenever he sends the copper chain,
it shall be the message of peace to the whole race.

"If enemies shall plot against you, he will know it, and
he will warn you by a messenger with the copper chain.

"If he shall need you to help him against an enemy, he
will send you a messenger with the copper chain.

"Whenever he shall send you the copper chain, it shall
be a sign of friendship, brotherhood, and peace. Massasoit
will be true to the gift of the copper chain!"

He went away, Governor Carver escorting him down
to the brook where the two embraced and parted.

The people now looked for Edward Winslow's return,
but instead came Quadequina.

The prince was young and of noble bearing. He started
in alarm as the trumpet sounded.

The muskets rattled again.

"Put them away," he said; "I like them not."

The men laid down their muskets, and the prince sat
down, probably on the green mat of good Mistress Winslow.

Poets have sung of the field of the cloth of gold, and painters have vied with each other in bringing back that romantic scene. But more to the world than the grand display of wealth, jewels, and personal splendor that took place when Henry VIII met Francis I on the field of the cloth of gold in 1520, just one hundred years before, were Mistress Elizabeth Winslow's green rug, and the matters that were concluded on it that March day at New Plymouth, and more in value to the English and French races than all the jewels of Henry and Francis, and of the glittering courts of England and France, was that copper chain, which proved a talisman to the Pilgrims, and protected the nation of the West as it lay in its cradle waiting to rise and lead a new world.

The day should be recalled by the history classes of our schools: Thursday, March 22, 1621. The copper chain was the wampum belt of New England, and it represents that nobility which is common to the better heart of the races of men.

It was the last day, we may suppose, that Mistress Elizabeth Winslow took part in any event of this changeable world, if indeed she were there.

The reaction of the awful voyage upon the sea seems never to have left her. The common disease which had spared her long was now upon her, just as the birds were singing, the arbutus blooming, and she had seen, as we may hope, the King of Pokonoket sit down on her green mat, and conclude the treaty of peace that would protect her husband and make her household treasure immortal.

When Edward Winslow returned from being hostage he saw that she was failing. He told her all the things that happened while he was " on the other side of the brook."

Ellen More sat beside her as the fever did its work. She must have been glad that she came. She had lived to see the bow of promise on the cloud.

Lovely Elizabeth Winslow died on March 24, 1621, two days after the treaty of peace. And Ellen More wept by the still, white form, and wondered if on the great ship of life the Pilot were still on board.

# CHAPTER XXIII.

### DEATH OF ELLEN MORE.

It is beautiful weather now, but the sickness in the colony has not ended.

The coming of Massasoit and the death of Mistress Elizabeth Winslow had brightened and darkened the life of little Ellen More. Her heart went out to Pilot Coppin in her loneliness. She drooped, and one spring day she did not come out of Edward Winslow's house, but sent word to the Billingtons in the Common House that she was ill and wished to see Pilot Coppin once more.

"John, you go and signal for him," said Mistress Billington: "the pilot is proper attached to the child. I wouldn't wonder if she had the same complaint as Mistress Winslow had; with frail people it follows a hard voyage, sooner or later. Her two little brothers have died of it, but her brother Richard seems to be strong. Go, John; I don't believe that you will have to go again."

John Billington, the lad, was never slow to do anything for little Ellen More. He signaled to the ship from the hill, and was answered by the Pilot, who knew the sign, and who soon came to the shore in a boat, where he was met by John.

"Ellen is sick," said the latter, "and wants to see you. She is at her home, the Winslow house."

"It is the last time," said Pilot Coppin. "I have seen her growing thin, and a little fever will carry her off. She will follow Mistress Winslow—I feel that will be so—I saw the disease coming, when she held my hand as Massasoit sat on the green mat."

The pilot went to the house of Edward Winslow, and there found Ellen waiting most anxiously for him to come.

"O pilot, pilot," said Ellen, "I was afraid that you would not get here in time. I am going away."

"Where, where, my Ellen?"

"Where Jasper went, where Mistress Winslow has gone. Do you know what happened when they buried Mistress Winslow? It was in the daytime. The birds were singing, and her grave was surrounded by flowers. Here are some of them—no mayflowers of Holland ever smelled so sweet as these, and they blossomed amid the snow. I like the birds that sing in the storm when the light is breaking in the cloud, and I love these little ground flowers that blossom amid the snow."

She tried to reach some of the mayflowers that stood in a bowl on a board, but she fell back on the bed saying:

"I am so tired, I feel more and more tired—I shall fall asleep soon, and then I will go away after the rest."

Pilot Coppin took her little hand and covered it with his two hard hands.

"Pilot, I have something that I want to say before I fall to sleep and go away. You have a silver pipe."

"Yes, yes, little one; it was a present to me."

"The Indians smoke when they make treaties of peace, do they not? Massasoit did; they said that Indians always do. It is their custom to smoke when they sit down to make peace."

"So I have been told."

"Pilot, I love Massasoit; he has a good spirit; he sees God in the sky, and in the forests, and everywhere, and he wants to do right. Did you see the look on his face when he said that the treaty that he agreed to keep was right? It was a look of the Great Spirit."

"Yes, I never could have believed that the face of a savage could have that light; but it did, Ellen, it did."

"Did you see how he trembled when he sat on the mat, and how the prince shook when the trumpet was blown? Pilot Coppin, I want you to do one thing more for me. Oh, you have been so good to me, so good. I can go away now that you are here—the Pilot is on board."

"Not the Great Pilot, Ellen."

"Yes, he is on board, too."

"What is it, Ellen? What do you want me to do?"

"I want that you should give to Massasoit the silver

pipe. Let John carry it to him; the people do not like John, but he has been good to me."

"I will let Tusquantum carry it to him, Ellen."

"Let John go with him."

"If Mistress Billington will."

"She is not liked here, but she, too, was always good to me. What you say makes me happy, Pilot Coppin. I am going to sleep now. You hold my hand while I sleep. You will know when I go away."

Her eyes closed. She was indeed very, very tired. Edward Winslow came into the curtained room and stood silent for a time, and then he said:

"My little orphan girl is almost through, Pilot Coppin. I am glad that you can be here. You had her heart."

Ellen began to breathe lightly, and her heart beat slowly.

It was a mild spring day, and the birds were singing without.

John Billington, the boy, came to inquire about Ellen. He brought some arbutus flowers from the brook where they grew profusely. The arbutus was the flower of the Pilgrims; it came amid the snow, as the iris to the cloud, and it should be always entwined with Pilgrim memories.

Ellen again and again seemed to have gone away, but life fluttered, like a bird's wing, and lingered.

She opened her eyes at last as in surprise.

"Pilot Coppin?"

"Yes, Ellen."

"I am going away now. All is well everywhere, Pilot Coppin. You are here—and the Great Pilot, he will pilot you, too; the Pilot is on board."

She fell asleep, and went away amid the odors of the mayflowers.

The pilot lifted the curtain of the little sleeping room and came out into the common room. John was there, and Edward Winslow sat before the fire.

"Ellen has gone," he said. "John, go with me and let me tell your mother. She has a good heart for such times as these. Heaven only knows how I loved that child. I am ready to sail now. She wanted that I should give my silver pipe to Massasoit. That I am going to do, and then I will wait to sail. I never shall forget that little heart, it is a spirit now—Ellen More, Ellen More!"

They buried her in the warm light of the vernal sky in the open earth, for there was now no longer any fear of Indians or of wolves.

Pilot Coppin brought the silver pipe from the ship, and when the little grave had closed he took it to the Common House.

"There remains but one thing more for me to do," he said to Mistress Billington. "I must do it before we sail, for the April weather is in the skies, and Master Jones says that we must soon away. I am going to carry the silver pipe which the traders gave me to Squanto, and send it by him to Massasoit, and give it to him in the name of

14

James, his brother king over the sea. I want John to go
with me—I am doing this for Ellen's sake."

"And it is loth I would be to hinder either of you from
obeying the wishes of the dead," said Mistress Billington.

The two went away to find Squanto, who had his dwell-
ing on one of the inland clearings where were fields of
maize.

The streams were flowing free, and yellow cowslips
lined their banks. The wild geese were coming back and
the few Indians who came here were preparing to plant
corn.

"It is a beautiful country," said the pilot, "and I would
be glad to remain with you here, but in a few days I shall
be on the sea again."

They found Squanto, and gave into his keeping the
silver pipe.

"I will take it to Ousamequin [Massasoit]," he said,
"and tell him that the pilot of the great ship has sent it to
him in the name of the English king. Master Coppin, do
you know what he will do with the silver pipe?"

"No, what, Tusquantum?"

"He will keep it until he finds one of his sagamores
or warriors who has done some deed nobler than he has
done, then he will send it to him. That is the rule of the
great Massasoit—that the noblest shall have the best. He
is no common chieftain; he has a big heart, and the eye
of the heart that sees what is right. This is not a treaty

present like the copper chain—that he will keep forever, and give to those who follow him. But this silver pipe, this will be buried in his grave, and laid on his heart there, or else, if he find that one of his sagamores has done a deed of the soul, he will send it to him, as to one more worthy than he to keep the treasure. He loves to reward deeds of the soul."

Squanto turned to John Billington.

" Son of the men of the Mayflower, you are yet young; you have met noble men in your own land, but none of them has more value in his spirit than our king of the forests, whose kingdom is Pokonoket, whose town is So-wams, and whose royal seat is at the burying ground of his race at Mount Hop [Hope]. You may live to learn lessons of virtue and honor some day from the Indian king. Your own people will do well if they will obey the law of justice that is ours. I hope some day, boy, to meet you again."

He did.

" John Billington," said the pilot, " if ever you should hear of the silver pipe again, write to me at my Scottish home over the sea."

" That I will be ready to do, Pilot Coppin. I think that you have planted a good seed in the silver pipe, though I know not how it will happen. It will be many a year before we shall forget you, Pilot Coppin, and I will write to you if good befall us after you are gone."

"Or if evil befall you, I will wish to hear all." He added: "John, we all have our work to do in life. No wind stirs the leaves in vain, nor does any keel vainly plow a single furrow of the sea. I feel as though it was the hand of Providence that made me the pilot of the May-flower, and that even the little life of Ellen More was not given to the world and the wilderness home for nought!"

The pilot looked upon the little settlement, and the ship with lifting sails.

"These people are founding a nation," he said, "who will make men their rulers, as they elected Governor Carver. When they landed here they agreed that each family should erect its own house, and all should build a Common House. Other people will come here, and the colony will grow, and build on in that way. It is the true way to found a nation in the will of the people. I can see the nation that is to be in the pattern that these exiles have made."

The pilot had the true vision.

# CHAPTER XXIV.

"THE boat from the Mayflower is coming in again!" said John Alden to Miles Standish one day in early spring. "What brings her back, I wonder? She flies the flag, and Captain Jones is on board. Robert Coppin is with him."

"It is almost time for her to sail," said Miles Standish, "and Captain Jones has long been weary of us and the new land. But he has grown more kindly toward us of late. Yes, the captain is on board the boat."

The two stood on the high ground of the town, and watched the boat as it approached the land.

It was an early spring day. The sky was warmer and bluer than they had ever seen it before. The wild geese were honking high in the mild, serene air. The bluebirds were on the wing, and the sea glimmered with flocks of joyous wings.

The boat touched the shore, and Captain Jones and Robert Coppin came up to the Common House. Standish went to meet them.

"The weather is fine," said the captain to Miles Standish, "so fine that we must be going now. The men are already trimming the sails, and it will be up anchor soon. Standish, do you want to know why I have come?"

"You have grown mellow of late, Captain Jones. I mind me that you have come to offer to take back letters and gifts to our people at home."

"Marry, my good friend. That I have, and better than that. I have come to offer to carry back any of the company who wish to return to England. Standish, I have been so much with these people that I pity them. It would be better for the weak women and the children to return. I have seen such people die until my heart has turned sick. Send for the governor and let me talk with him. I will go into the Common House and wait."

Richard More, the lad "put out" to the Brewster family, was near.

"Richard," said Captain Jones, "go and call the elder. Tell him that Captain Jones is at the Common House, and has a message for him."

John Alden, who had been with Miles Standish, went away to ask the attendance of Governor Carver at the Common House.

The captain stood in the sunny door of the Common House and looked out over Burial Hill.

"Half of your people lie there," he said to Standish, "without so much as one gravestone. You are going to plant that field of the dead, I am told. O Standish, Standish, think what those poor people suffered! May I never see the like of it again. In God's name send the orphans back with me. Let Leyden, where they were born, shelter them again. Let John Robinson care for them. At least let Mary Allerton and Remember Allerton return."

Governor Carver came out of his house and was soon at the door of the Common House. He was followed by Bradford and Elder Brewster. These men with Standish and John Alden sat down together in the house.

"Governor Bradford, I am getting ready to sail, and to leave you alone in the wilderness. I am not so hard a man as I was. I have come to respect this colony, to love the people and to pity them. I know the secret of Burial Hill. Governor, I am willing to take you and your people back again."

"I am touched by your kindness, Captain Jones, but I have no wish to return. How is it with you, Elder Brewster? I would not prevent any one from returning who wishes to go, but while there is any hope of founding a colony here, where men may be free, I must remain here. I, too, know the secrets of Burial Hill."

"I have no wish to return," said Elder Brewster. "While there is any hope that we may found a colony where faith may be free, I must remain here. I, too, know the secrets of Burial Hill."

"My place is here," said Miles Standish, and at the word "here" he struck the floor with his magic sword.

"Here I remain," said John Alden.

"And with you all here will I live and die," said William Bradford.

"But Captain Jones has shown no ordinary nature in this thing," said the governor. "Miles Standish, sound the trumpet, and call all of the people together and let me tell them what the captain has said."

The trumpet was sounded from the door. In a short time nearly fifty of the hundred and two people who sailed from Delft for the new land sat down on the log benches, wondering what had caused the trumpet to be sounded.

"Speak for me, Elder Brewster," said the governor.

The elder arose and bent forward.

"My people, you that are left—you, the remnant of my people, you that are left of the blessed company of John Robinson—hear!

"The Mayflower is about to sail. Your letters home must be finished at once. Captain Jones here will take them back, and it is a ready and willing spirit that he shows. But hear! The captain is willing to take you back to the old world, and to your old home. How many of you wish to go? As many as wish to go back to the old world again let them rise and stand, that we may dismiss you with our blessing."

No one arose. There was a deep silence. A future destiny was in the silence.

"The wilderness may be stormy," said Stephen Hopkins, "but that old world, that old world is stormier! No, no, whatever may happen to me and mine, let me live and die here, where there is hope for mankind."

"Edward Winslow," said Elder Brewster, "what say you?"

"I must live in free air," said the great traveler, "I and mine. We have seen many graves open and close here, but I have no wish to return."

"Remember Allerton, orphan, what say you?"

"I have no wish to leave my mother's grave, and the place of her dearest wishes for the welfare of our company."

"Mary Allerton, orphan?"

"I have no desire to go back. I wish to live with those who have suffered and survived."

"Priscilla Mullins, you, too, are an orphan, and the graves of both of your parents are here. What say you?"

"'Where thou livest, I will live!'"

"Elizabeth Tilley? Thou, too, art an orphan. Thy father and mother sleep with the rest."

"'Where thou diest, I will die!'"

"Mary Chilton? Thou wert among the first of the women to land on this rocky shore. Thy father died on the Mayflower, in the harbor, and thy mother perished here in the dark days of the storm. What sayest thou?"

"It is the answer of Ruth, the Moabitess, that I, too,

would return. I, who was among the first to step upon these shores, would be the last to leave. I speak from the heart, and my voice is like the others. Let me live here, and die here, and be laid in the earth beside my parents who gave their all for this cause!"

Tears were flowing.

There was a long silence. They had made their decision. It was the first election in America.

Then Robert Coppin rose up.

"You are all unwilling to leave this new free land. I must go; I would that I could stay. Send your messages home by me, and say of me that I was ever true to you, and that I loved you."

"Pilot Coppin has been true," said they all.

He went toward the door.

"Let me go once more to the spot where Ellen More lies buried."

The company talked an hour or more, then Captain Jones and Robert Coppin went down to the boat, and were rowed out to the Mayflower, bearing letters and messages.

The next morning in the red light of the sun the ship spread her sails. The women went up on Burial Hill to see her lift her anchor, put out the flag of their old land, and move slowly, slowly, into the dim distances of the blue air and sea. She bore away one heart that all loved—it was that of Robert Coppin, "our pilot."

The ship was leaving three thousand miles of empty ocean behind her, but the wide sea was to be a defense to the Pilgrim colony.  The great republic could have been planted as well in no other place and in no other way.  It is faith and obstacles that produce power.

# CHAPTER XXV.

## LOST.

"Blow the trumpet! Do something! Oh, my heart is clean gone. Blow!"

It was a summer day; the sky was full of birds, the forests of leaves, and the whole country bright with berries and flowers.

There was excitement in the Common House. John Billington, the lad, liked to wander afar into the forest, but he usually returned at night. He had been gone two days now, and it was nearing the nightfall of the third day.

Mistress Billington was given to scolding John, but she loved him, and now that he did not come back she moved about from place to place in nervous agitation.

"Miles Standish," she said, "where do you think John, my John, has gone?"

"The Indians may have got him!"

"Don't say that. This mortar pestle is harder than your head, but not harder than your heart. Don't you turn on me, captain though you are—I'm not a woman to take any sarse from you. If the Indians have got him they will return him—I would as soon trust him to their mercies as to yours. Is Tusquantum here?"

"Yes, Mistress Fliptongue."

"Then send him to me. My b'ye [boy], my b'ye, he will find my b'ye! Go! go! Night is coming on. If he don't come back to-night not a wink of sleep will I have. I'll wander, I'll howl, I'll cry out to the top of the heavens. Go! go! You don't know a mother's feelings—you haven't any feelings anyhow. Your heart is a wooden clapper. Go! You may command the musketeers, but I rule here in the block house. If any Indians have done harm to my b'ye, it is because you have hardened them to do it by your show of authority."

"I enforce the law as a lawful subject of King James—nothing more."

"King James owns nothing on this side of the water."

"Who does?"

"Not he, nor you, nor Governor Bradford. The Indians own the land. If they had discovered you, would they have owned you? But this is neither here nor there. My b'ye, my b'ye!"

Miles Standish might under other circumstances have threatened the poor woman with arrest as a shrew, but he did not stop to argue more now. He saw her baking manchets in a wild way, now running to the manchets at the fire, now to the door, now sending for Dr. Fuller, now for the trumpeter, and he merely said:

"The woman is distracted. I will send out a hunting party to-morrow if the boy does not come back. The Billingtons are always in trouble, but the boy must be found."

The summer night came and passed, but the boy did not come back. Mistress Billington met Miles Standish at the door in the morning.

"I haven't slept a wink to-night. I'm mad, Miles Standish, mad. Now what are you going to do with me?"

"Find the boy. I've got a party together already, and Squanto is going with them. You may go on baking manchets, Mistress Billington; if the boy is with the Indians, he is safe, and Squanto will find him."

"If he is with any of Massasoit's Indians he is safe," said Mistress Billington. "I would trust that king as soon as I would King James."

The trumpet blew. The party formed by Miles Standish were ready to go into the forests along the shore, by the way of a boat, which would enable them to explore the coast and the woods.

Mistress Billington shrieked when she heard the trumpet, then she became calm, and went on with her cooking of fish and baking of manchets. She had many mouths to provide for and few to help her.

She went to the door from time to time to listen. Before her lay cornfields glimmering in the sun. Squanto had showed the settlers how to plant the fields, putting alewives into the hills of corn. Squanto had taught the colonists many things beside fertilizing the plowed earth with alewives—as how to tread eels out of the mud in springtime, how to plant beans, and ensnare water fowl. He was the man of "good cheer" in the colony now that Pilot Coppin had gone.

The party with Squanto went to Nauset [Eastham], where dwelt Aspinet, who was a friend of Massassoit, and probably one of the latter's sagamores. On their way, night coming on, they stopped at Cummaquid. There they met one of the most amiable Indians of whom we have any record, Yanough. Mourt says of him that he "was very personable, gentle, courteous and fair conditioned, and not like a savage save for his attire."

The English inquired if a white boy had been seen at Cummaquid.

"He is safe," said the chief of Cummaquid. "But he is not here; he is at Nauset. Rest with us, and I will guide you to him."

The chief made a feast for the hungry strangers, and set his people to serving them. He was a young man, and had a fine courtesy with his hospitality. The English wondered that such a heart could be found in a savage.

A strange thing happened while the English were being entertained here by the amiable sachem. There had been lost boys in this country before John Billington went astray.

The strange happening was very dramatic, and it is

briefly told by Mourt in his Narration. We might make a story of it, but we will quote it here from Mourt in its original simplicity. The old writer says:

"One thing was very grievous unto us at this place. There was an old woman, whom we judged to be no less than a hundred years old; which came to see us because she never saw English [before]; yet could not behold us, without breaking forth into [a] great passion, weeping and crying excessively. We demanding the reason of it; they told us, She had three sons, who, when Master Hunt was in these parts, went aboard his ship to trade with him; and he carried them captives into Spain, for Tusquantum at that time was carried away also: by which means, she was deprived of the comfort of her children in her old age.

We told them, "We were sorry that any Englishman should give them that offense; that Hunt was a bad man, and that all the English that heard of it condemned him for the same: but for us, we would not offer them any such injury; though it would gain us all the skins in the country. So we gave her some small trifles, which somewhat appeased her."

It was as hard for this old woman to lose her whole family as for nervous Mistress Billington to be parted from John. There are episodes in which the simple narrative is better than any of the lights of fiction, and this is one.

These Indians were those that attacked the English at the time of the exploration from Provincetown. Can

it be wondered at that they should have regarded the explorers as enemies after having had some of their own
people stolen by the crew of an English ship like the Mayflower?

Strange as it may seem, Squanto had been carried away
by the same adventurers that had taken the old woman's
sons.

"I pity you," said Squanto to the ancient Indian. "But
these white people are not like those. They are your
friends, and the others are your enemies."

The words were kindly, but they did not bring back her
sons to comfort her in her lonely old age.

The original narrative of Mourt thus pictures the con-
tinuance of the journey:

"We took boat to Nauset, Iyanough and two of his
men accompanying us. Ere we came to Nauset, the day
and tide were almost spent, insomuch as we could not go
in with our shallop: but the Sachem or Governor Cummaquid went ashore, and his men with him. We also sent
Tusquantum to tell Aspinet, the Sachem of Nauset, where-
fore we came."

While in this interesting country, where they had first
landed, they found the owners of the corn that they had
taken for their necessities in the winter. They arranged
to pay them for it, and did so to the satisfaction of the
owners of the ground barns.

Tusquantum hurried forward to Nauset to Aspinet, and
15

told the chieftain his errand. The Indian was pleased to receive the messenger from the English, and to learn that the latter were on their way to his country. He sent for the boy. John Billington came to the royal residence, accompanied by warriors.

"Tusquantum," he said, "you have been true to me. I never thought to meet you here. I did not mean to run away from Plymouth. I got lost in the woods, and when I thought I was travelling toward home, I was going away from it. Tusquantum, do you remember that silver pipe, and what you said to me then? Let me go back with you."

"Boy, the English are coming for you in a boat."

"Let us make the English happy when they see how we have used their lost boy," said Aspinet. "English boy, come here. Your friends are coming for you. Let me put on your neck a string of my beads, and cover you with our own ornaments."

They dressed the boy as though he was one of the royal family, or as for a harvest dance.

Then Aspinet summoned his warriors, a hundred in number, and mounted the boy on the back of one of his men of great stature, and they marched down to the sea.

The boat was in sight, but in shoal water, far from the land.

They carried the boy out to the boat, bedecked like a

*The return of the lost boy.*

young chief. The party wondered indeed when they saw him safe and so arrayed and attended.

And happy was Mistress Billington when the boy came running to the Common House in his royal apparel.

"I never will say 'scat' again to any Indian. It is hard to tell in this world who are our friends or who are our enemies. Our life is all full of misunderstandings, and sometimes I think that all people mean well, only all are alike blind, and we do not follow the teaching of the Sermon on the Mount as we used to do. I sometimes feel just as I should not, and I mean to be a better woman now that John has come home. Sit down, John, and tell us all about where you have been, and where Squanto found you. You used to say that you wanted to become an Indian chief, and now you do look like one, indeed. What would Pilot Coppin say were he to see you now?"

Pilot Coppin? He was on the docks of London or Southampton, or perhaps in his old home near Glasgow now.

John told his story.

"So the Indians have returned a lost boy to the white race who have robbed them of their own boys," said good Elder Brewster. "That is noble."

"You ought to tell Massasoit of that," said Mistress Billington to Squanto. "Perhaps you will."

"I will tell the King of Pokonoket what Aspinet has done," said Squanto. "I am going to Sowams, where he lives, and he shall know it all. He will send Aspinet some gift. It was a deed worthy of a chain. Aspinet took off his own chain and gave it to the boy."

"It may be that Massasoit will send to Aspinet the copper chain," said Elder Brewster.

"No, he would never do that," said Squanto. "That chain is a pledge—a treaty chain—he would never do that! He would send him some other present—it may be that we shall some time find the heart of Massasoit in this thing. This is a deed of the spirit. It is the deeds of the soul that please him well."

"Miles Standish," said Mistress Billington, "would you be as magnanimous as that?"

"Now that your boy has returned you will have to command your tongue better than of late, Mistress Billington, or I will have to ask Governor Bradford to command you."

"The land of Goshen! Well, let time tell which of us is right; time tells the truth about all things, so I need have nothing more to say."

The Pilgrims were very thoughtful that night. They assembled in the Common House and sang some psalms from the old Ainsworth collection, John Howland, who sang in the storm, leading the voices. Then they went out. The whip-poor-wills were filling the woods with their mournful notes. Fireflies were in the woodland pastures. The great moon hung over the harbor and shone on the level graves on the hill, and on the brook and the fields of corn below.

The air was full of odor, now that the dew was falling. The wild rose and sweetbrier grew everywhere; there were laurels and sweet ferns on the rocks, and marsh flowers on the borders of the sea.

A dark form passed westward in the moonlight. It was Tusquantum.

"Good night," he said to the men as he was about to cross the brook. "It is cooler traveling at night. I am going to Pokonoket—it is a friendly message that I will bear to Massassoit. Tusquantum will come back again!"

The doors of the seven houses opened and closed, and all was as silent in Plymouth town as was the moonlit burying place on the hill.

# CHAPTER XXVI.

## THE WHITE FOOL KING.

OCTOBER was at hand. The red leaves began to hang like banners on the trees. The cool wind strewed the by-ways with leaves, and there were gatherings of flocks of birds in the old Indian cornfields. The leaves of the corn rustled in the Pilgrims' fields. The nights with the coppery moon of the fading year grew long again.

Mistress Billington began to kindle chimney fires again in the Common House, and the people gathered there at night and recalled the dark winter of death, and told over the stories of the terrible voyage, and recalled Good Cheer Coppin and Captain Jones, who, notwithstanding an unproved suspicion that he purposely landed them at Cape Cod, was so very good to them in the winter of their sufferings that they liked to think of him now.

One night in the middle autumn all the old voyagers in New Plymouth met at the Common House. Mistress Billington made for them nocake and served it with a delicious sauce of berries.

Suddenly the door opened and Squanto appeared. He was indeed the tongue of the English, and he was always welcome. He was the story-teller now that Pilot Coppin had gone.

"I've wonder to tell," said he, when only halfway across the room. "You that have ears give them to me."

"What is it?" asked Governor Brewster. "Has a ship been seen?"

"No, no, it relates to John Billington here. Massasoit has given the silver pipe to the sannap who rescued the boy."

"Why should he do that?" asked Governor Bradford.

"It was no common deed. The English once stole the boys of the tribe that rescued him, and you sent your captain against Corbitant when you thought he was plotting against Massasoit."

"How wonderful," said Elder Brewster. "Love brings love and hatred hatred, and to forgive is to be forgiven. Massasoit is our Melchizedek. We may well pay tribute to him. Such a man is without father or mother, without beginning of years or end of days."

"Would you have done as well, Miles Standish?" said Brewster reprovingly. "Be a little careful, a little careful; your ways in Flanders were sometimes hard. Does it not shame us to find among pagans such a man as Yanough?"

Squanto took his place among those who read fortunes in the fire, or at least saw pictures there. He was asked to tell some tale of this land of Pawtuxet, in which he was the only survivor of the plague.

"The sachem of Nauset had a sister once," he said, and then paused. He continued in Indian narrative style: "She wanders; she wails with the winds; she cries when the winds bite and the wolf howls. She married the White King Fool."

These words startled the company.

"Who was the White King Fool?" asked Edward Winslow.

Priscilla Mullins and Mary Chilton locked arms and stood close to Squanto. The young folks gathered closely around him.

"Let me poke the fire first," said Mistress Billington, "sith the tale will be a still one, then you may begin."

She poked the fire and the sparks flew.

"The Indians' memories are long," he began, "and the Nausets have much to remember; but to hearts that are kind the Nauset is kind, and his heart melts for those who do him well.

"It was moons ago in winter. The Nausets were housed in their cabins, and telling smoke talk tales and parching and pounding their corn.

"A runner came. His breath was spent.

"'Out, out!' he cried. 'There's a great bird lit on the sea!'

"The Nausets ran out of their tents. A monster was in full view on the ocean with spread wings. It was a ship, but they had never seen a ship like that before. It was not like that that carried their boys away.

"The monster seemed fighting with the storm. But the storm's wings were bigger than its own; the storm drove the monster into the shoals and upon the rocks, and as many men as you have fingers came trembling in from the sea.

"The Nausets saw them. They watched them. They said:

"'The sea has sent them to us for us to punish them for stealing our people who never came back again.'

"The men were white. They made themselves shelters, and found food in the sea.

"The Nausets watched them.

"One day they fell upon them with a whoop that startled the wind. They captured them all and carried them away.

"'Now,' said the Nausets, 'we will be revenged upon them for those who stole our people, who never came back.'

"Would they kill them? No. Would they make them work in their fields? No. What would they do with them? They would make 'fools' of them; they would send them around as presents to the sagamores to make sport for the people, as little foxes make sport, as the tame blue jays make sport, as the papooses make sport.

"So they sent the white fool men as gifts to the sagamores.

"The sachem of Nauset's sister was young and very

handsome.   Her eyes were black and sparkled, her cheeks were soft and clear.   She was the light of the tribe.

"Now one of the white fool men was young.   He had white hair, his eyes were blue, his form was straight.   The Indians loved to look upon him when he did fool tricks for them.

"He came from the land called France.   I have seen the land.   It is very warm and fair.

"The princess loved to see this man, whom they called France, make sport.   Every day she asked her brother the king to send for him.

"There were young braves who loved the princess, and they wrestled with him, and leaped with him, and performed many antics with him, that she might admire them.

"But it was not these she began to admire; it was France, for a soft heart had this same princess.

"One day there was to be a feast, and the princess asked her brother the king to bring out the young man France again for sport.

"It was to be a great feast and she said:

"'We must have high sport to-day.   What shall the game be?'

"'The feathering of the tree,' said the king.

"She shrank back.   'Not that, not that,' she said.

"'Why not?' asked the king.   'That is the finest sport of all.'

"The feathering of the tree was to bind a noble form

to a tree, and to shoot arrows at the tree, to show how near to the form they might strike the wood and yet not hit the man. When the sport was over the tree would be found pictured with feathers, and if the braves had shot well, the bound man would escape, leaving his picture in the form of arrows sticking into the tree. But if a bowstring went wrong, when the arrows flew near the breast or the head, the captive was wounded or fell dead.

"It was high noon in the forests on the edge of the sea. The young man France had been bound against the trunk of an old oak, and to the braves who were to show their skill places were assigned by the king.

"'The bowman who shall shoot his arrow nearest to the mark and leave the captive unharmed shall be taken into my council, and be honored by me above the others,' said the king.

"There were lovers of the princess among the braves. It was understood that the one who sent his arrow nearest to the captive and left him unharmed would be favored by the king as the winner of the princess.

"The shooting began at the foot of the tree. The princess stood in her tent, more beautiful, it seemed, than ever before.

"The arrows feathered the tree at the feet of the captive. Then they ran up the tree one by one, and fell under his arms, near his heart. Not an arrow drew a drop of blood.

"Then they feathered the oak above the captive's shoulders, when one arrow struck through his hair.

"When the princess saw this she rushed out to the tree. Another arrow grazed the captive's cheek.

"'I will see how near to his eye I can lodge an arrow,' said a young warrior, filled with hope at the appearance of the princess.

"The princess rushed upon the raised bow and seized the bowman's hand.

"'Never!' she cried. 'I have given my heart to him. I will make him my chief—unbind the cords!'

"They unbound the captive, and she led him away to her tent. In a few moons she was married to him, and the braves of other tribes came to call him the 'Fool King.'

"A child was born to them, and they lived in happiness in their tent, and roamed the woods together. But the sickness of the land fell upon him and he died, and the child died with him at the time.

"The princess saw them buried in one grave, and then her heart broke and her mind gave way. She rushed into the forests and wandered away. They thought that she went to the rescue of the other white captives, who had been made fool men. But she never came back. They saw her flying from place to place, but she heeded no one's call. They hear her at times on windy nights when wolves cry and winds are out, but her cry is like the winds.

"She used to come back alone to the White King's

grave. They sometimes saw her fleeing away in the morning, but she never visited her people. Then she was lost to every one, and they heard her voice no more. If you will go with me I will show you the tree that was feathered on the day of the feast. The Indian girl's heart is true, and Death is cruel when he slays the one she loves. She loves to be a slave to the one to whom she gives her heart."

The Pilgrims listened to the legend, and pitied the princess who cried in the storm.

Then they talked of their loved ones in England and Holland; of John Robinson, of the people who were waiting to come. They talked of their own loved ones who were sleeping on the hill, of Rose Standish and Ellen More.

Then John Billington, the lad, said:

"I am going to write to our pilot to-morrow, to Good Cheer Coppin."

"That is right, boy," said Elder Brewster. "Send him my message of good cheer; may he find other ports for the exiles of the world."

"Say to him good cheer for me," said Edward Winslow. "I well remember how he rose up in the boat on that awful day, and shouted 'Good cheer! I see a harbor!'"

"So do I," said Governor Bradford. "Tell him, boy, Governor Bradford wishes him good cheer."

Then one after another said the same words, and John Howland led a company of singers in one of Ainsworth's psalms, as he had sung amid the raging waters when our pilot said, " I see a harbor! "

They wondered what Pilot Coppin would say when he read John's letter, and learned that the silver pipe had come back to the cape again.

# CHAPTER XXVII.

## THE COPPER CHAIN AGAIN.

IN the early fall, when the woods glowed with an unusual brightness and the old oaks began to wear a russet hue, Mistress Billington went out to a storehouse that had been built during the summer, carrying a pail of hot tallow in her hands. It was "dipping-candle" day with her; she had saved tallow from the animals for food after the early fall huntings, and with this she planned to have some good lights for the Common House in the late fall and winter to come.

She was about to enter the storehouse where a kettle had been set in the chimney, when she was seen to stop suddenly and to throw up one hand.

"Scat! scat! scamper, or I will pour the tallow all over you!"

She turned, and came running toward the Common House, spilling the hot tallow as she came. Her eyes protruded, and her face was flushed.

"Run!" she cried out to the men in the Common

House. "He stands there by the soap barrel. Run! O my eyes, O good pity, did I ever see the like!"

"What is it?" asked the men.

"The evil one of the woods," cried the excited woman. "You never saw his like. He is half Indian and half bear, and he has claws around his neck!"

The men hurried to the storehouse. They found there an Indian who presented a strange appearance indeed. He wore an apron of wild-cat skin, around his neck was a string of birds' claws, and half of his face was painted black. By his side was a pouch or bag of shells, and over his forehead waved a white plume.

He laughed, which brought out his white teeth prominently, and they contrasted curiously with his half black and half copper face.

The men beckoned him to follow them. He did so in a friendly way to the Common House.

When Mistress Billington saw him coming into the house her terrors were renewed. She turned around and around, and seizing the cooling tallow, threatened to make a candle of the Indian, but finally set it down before him, with her familiar expression, "The land of Goshen!" but followed it up with one equally scriptural, "He's an Amalekite!"

The Indian did not understand her terrors, but simply said, "Much squaw," having learned a few English words from some one, possibly Squanto. He added, "Truck, truck."

He took up the tallow stick and began to eat the cooling tallow, which caused the good woman to lift up her hands in astonishment.

"Much goodt!" he said.

The men tried to talk with him, but he did not comprehend what they would say. He simply said: "No ears," and called for Squanto, adding, "Truck, truck!"

Squanto had gone away to the hunting grounds.

The men thought that he might be a messenger.

They asked him whence he came, but received no answer that they could understand, except "Truck, truck!"

Then he thought of some English words.

"The little girl," he asked suddenly; "little spirit?"

"He means Ellen More," said Mistress Billington, softening and throwing her apron over her head at the thought of the sorrows of the never-to-be-forgotten spring.

"Gone," said she, pointing upward.

"Gorn?" echoed the Indian in a forlorn voice. "Little girl gorn?"

He sat down on the doorsill, and did not speak a word for a long time.

The men consulted together, as the last rays of the sun sprinkled the hills. They pointed him to the woods and motioned him away.

He rose up and shook his head: "Truck!"

"Indian go now," said one of the men pointing to the sunset.

16

He again shook his head, but stood like a statue:
" Truck! "

Then one of the men attempted to lead him down to the
brook. But he refused to go.

Another ordered him away with decisive gestures.

He put his hand into his bag of shells, and drew something out very carefully. It gleamed. It was the copper
chain.

" He has been sent by Massasoit," said Mistress Billington. " Let him come in again."

They gave him a place by the fire.

" I wish the green mat were here," said Mistress Billington, " and I would that Mistress Winslow and Ellen were
here, which they will never be again. The Indian is a messenger of peace, and his paint is meant for ornament. I
think the black paint is intended to make whiter his plume."

She called him " White Plume " now, and hurried
about to get a supper for him. She was full of bustle to
serve him, and was sorry for her first treatment of him.

The Pilgrims' hearts melted when they saw the copper
chain. The old days of the voyage came back to them
again, with thoughts of the pilot and the little grave on the
hill.

In the evening Squanto came back to the Common
House. He talked for a time with the Indian, when his
errand was made clear.

Massasoit desired to send a party of Indians to *truck*

with the Pilgrims—that is, to sell furs. Massasoit would like to visit the English again, when the leaves were falling.

They spread a mat for the white-plumed messenger by the fire.

Then they talked of "our pilot" who had gone over the sea, of Ellen More and the copper chain, and they wished that the "little spirit" could have been there to have seen the beginning of the mission of peace of that little present that had been brought to the great and generous forest king.

The copper chain went about from place to place on messages like this. Wherever any Indian bore it, and held it up to glimmer in the sun, there was amity, good will, and peace. The Mayflower brought no treasure that was equal in noble influence to the copper chain.

# CHAPTER XXVIII.

## THE FIRST THANKSGIVING.

It was one that can never be repeated. It may be painted from the imagination, and sung in song, and acted in tableau, but the race is gone that made that festival a thrilling scene. The Pilgrims had produced their first harvest on American soil. They must return thanks to God for the bounty of the fields, and for the promise that the harvest gave them of harvests yet to come. The Indians had protected them after the promise that Massasoit had made when he received the copper chain. They must invite the Indians to their feast; they must send for the good Massasoit; the monarch of the forest must come back to them bringing the copper chain.

Says Bradford of the Pilgrims at this time: "They began now to gather in ye small that they had, and to fit up their houses and dwellings against winter, being all well recovered in health and strength, and had all things in good plenty."

It was Indian summer, the time of the serenity of the woods. The cranberry meadows were turning red, and their borders were lined with purple gentians. Wild grapes hung from the oaks and junipers, under the fluttering leaves, which had turned yellow. The birds were gathering in flocks, and the ospreys had gone away from their nests of sticks of wood piled high on the dead trees.

Governor Bradford called his men who were most swift of foot to his house one day.

"Go to Sowams in the Pokonoket country," said he, "and inquire for Massasoit. If he be there, tell him that we are now ready to receive him; invite him to come with his chief men to partake of the Thanksgiving feast with us. If he be not there, find him. He may be at the gathering of harvest on the Mt. Hope Lands, or at the fishing grounds on one of the rivers."

The men departed gladly. They were full of confidence in the heart of the grand old chieftain; they loved him. Every Indian on their way would bid them good speed when they told their errand.

Massasoit was the heart of his people.

With the Pilgrims all was preparation.

Hunters were sent out for deer and wild turkeys, for partridges, quail, and rabbits, of which the woods were full.

The chimneys of the thatched houses smoked. The kitchens were busy. The Brewster house was especially a scene of anticipation for the invited guests. Priscilla Mullins lived there.

It was Thursday, in the first days of November. The

samp, the probable succotash, the possible "nocake," and like dishes were made. The game was prepared for roasting. Massassoit had sent back word by the messengers that he would dine with Governor Bradford on that great day.

It was a still morning—so still that one might hear the leaves falling in the crystal air. The witch-hazels were blooming; like some lives they blossom in the fall. The woods were full of odors. The sun rose over the sea. The doors of the seven dwellings and four public houses were open, and the smoke of ovens rose from the seven chimneys.

A yell rent the air. The people stood still for a moment, then ran out of their houses.

"Massasoit is coming!" cried the sentinel.

Massasoit was indeed coming with the copper chain, and he was bringing with him ninety warriors.

The people gathered by the sides of the path that led to the governor's house, and waited to welcome the Indians as they should come marching in.

The Indians came plumed and painted, in cloaks ornamented with mystic figures, in bows and quivers, and circles of glittering wampum. By the side of Massasoit walked, as we may suppose, the stately Quadequina, his brother, who loved him, and was seldom absent from him. It may be that Annawon was there, for he lived to be very old. "Pnieses" were there, the Indian mystics, who thought that they held communion with the dead. Tusquantum was there, the interpreter.

The Indians, led by Massasoit, wearing the copper chain, marched down the hill to the governor's door, and were welcomed there by the governor.

The welcome was followed by the roll of a drum.

It was the signal for prayer.

They entered the meeting house.

All stood silent, the Indians following the example of the worshipers. Then Brewster, with uncovered head, returned thanks to God for the harvests of the year, for the amity of the Indians, for the promise and hope of the future. It was probably the first public prayer that the Indians had ever heard.

The feasts followed the services in the church.

Ninety warriors were many to feed, but ample preparations had doubtless been made.

The day was mild, and they spread the tables in the open air.

The Indians engaged in leaping and other feats of skill. Miles Standish led out his little company of twenty soldiers, and caused them to go through the customary drill.

The Indians yelled with delight as they witnessed the manœuvers of the soldiers. The scene was wholly new to them.

The Thanksgiving lasted three days, during which the English and Indians entered into a better understanding with each other, so as to part in the brotherhood of love and peace.

The last day of this memorable feast fell on Saturday. For this farewell meal the Pilgrim mothers had made their most bountiful and delicate dishes. The feast may have begun with puddings and nocake, and delicacies made of nuts, instead of ending with such things, as that was not an uncommon method of old colony times.

What did they have to eat on that day? Was their provision as good as that which could be made to-day? Probably, and better. The venison may have had rich stews and gravies; the wild turkeys may have been flavored with beechnuts; the clam chowder may have had rare relishes; the game of many kinds may have found that flavor of the home oven that no others can equal. The meal probably began or ended with plum porridge. Succotash was the great Indian dish, and that may have been provided with venison. Wild geese may have been served.

The Indians contributed to the meal. They brought oysters. That was probably the day of the first oyster stew ever eaten by white people on the New England coast.

It was the beautiful time of the year.

The forest, full of the odors of the fall, seemed to stand still in these last glorious days of the fading season.

The Pilgrims remembered the stormy voyage on those bright days; the terrible sickness; the burial of their loved ones at night under the white stars, or amid the drifting

snows. They remembered the sailing away of the Mayflower, leaving them there firm in the faith that they were
fulfilling the will of God.

We may well remember Elder Brewster's glorious words
at this period, as he bid the Pilgrims to be true to their purpose in the world, whatever might come:

" Blessed will it be for us, blessed for this land, for this
vast continent! Nay, from generation to generation will
the blessing descend. Generations to come will look back
to this hour and these scenes of agonizing trial, this day of
small things and say: ' Here was our beginning as a people.
These were our fathers. Through their trials we inherit
our blessings. Their faith is our faith; their hope our hope;
their God our God.' "

Such a voice as that in the wilderness is one for which
this nation should be thankful. We are what we are because
these heroes of faith were what they were. No record on
earth can surpass the scenes of that Pilgrim year, whose
faith bowed the skies, touched the heart of the savages, and
turned the wail of prayer into the Thanksgiving psalm in
the harvest suns of November. Faith is immortal power.

Massasoit went away, bearing the copper chain.

# CHAPTER XXIX.

## "GOOD CHEER!"

THE pilot of the Argo and of the Argonauts did not return from Colchis, where Jason had found the Golden Fleece. The fifty heroes of Greece with their fifty oars, who overcame the dragon, live on in fame; Orpheus forever sings in the remembrance of art, and Hercules still leads the inspirations of human achievement. But the man who piloted all has left small record in these golden dreams of fable.

It was so with our pilot, who said in the storm and the stress of the sea, "Good cheer!" The Mayflower came back again, but so far as we know he never returned. He left his word of "good cheer" in the New World, but he probably found an unmarked grave on some Scottish heather, or an unknown resting place in the sea.

But his words of good cheer did not die on the winds. The Faith Monument at Plymouth may not be the most artistic work of memorial art in America, but the lover of the spirit of history feels there, as he surveys the majestic face of stone uplifted to the skies, as he can feel nowhere else in the Western world. It is a statue with a soul, and

240

every true American should stand on the Plymouth Rock of Faith, and should sit down in the shadow of that colossal statue, and think of what Faith did in the sublime events that have made our history glorious in the achievements of character.   On Burial Hill and around it rest the men who bowed to the heavens, and sang in the storm, and saw the visions of destiny, to whom character was everything. They were precisioners indeed, but they held the faith of the heroes of Hebrew history; and Westminster Abbey has no nobler dust than is gathered here, amid these arbutus-blooming hills.   It is they who said, as interpreted by the poetic eloquence of Daniel Webster: " Advance then, ye future generations! "

A farewell glance at the humble Scottish pilot, who cheered the children of the Mayflower.

He sits on the docks of London.

" Pilot Coppin," says a shipmate, " there's a letter for you in the shipping office; it comes from over the sea."

The pilot hurries away for the letter.   He secures it and looks at it.

" It is from that boy, John Billington," he says.

He sits down in the sun, where the Thames rolls by, bearing outward and inward the argosies of the waters.

He reads with wonder the generous epistle, and claps his hands on his knees when he has put it away to read again.

It is a short message:

"Pilot Coppin—'Good Cheer': We are all happy now, and Squanto is with us. Massasoit has given the silver pipe to the sannap who rescued me when I was lost in the woods.

"O Pilot Coppin, how strange it all is! The Indians who had been robbed of their own people did not harm me; they rescued me, and they sent me back to my home with a chain about my neck. They were happy to do it.

"The people all wondered at it, and Massasoit gave the silver pipe to the Indian who found me when I was lost.

"We think of you, Pilot Coppin; we remember the jackscrew; we love to tell of the time when you cried 'Good cheer—I see a harbor!' Elder Brewster says that the harbor will welcome the pilgrims of the world.

"The people all tell me to say to you 'Good cheer' for them. So good cheer, good cheer forever, Pilot Coppin, and good-by, from your loving friend,

"JOHN BILLINGTON."


"Good cheer! good cheer!" repeated the pilot. "It cheers me now that I spoke those words out of the faith of my heart. Happy are they all who say 'good cheer' to the struggling world!"

He goes to St. Paul's Cathedral, and kneels down there on the stone floor among the poor people, and says, "Let me thank God for the faith of the Mayflower." He thinks of the words that had been given him in the storm, of little

Ellen More in her grave on Precisioners' Hill, and he rises up as the great bell peals, and goes out singing in the sunshine as his old comrade of the sea had sung in the storm.

Reader, it was Faith that made this nation what it is. Make a pilgrimage to Plymouth Rock, and in the faith of the American Argonauts face the new problems of life, and live for the things that live. There are few records of faith more tender and inspiring than the simple story of the children of the Mayflower.

# APPENDIX.

## THE PLYMOUTH OF TO-DAY.

WE repeat—every American should stand on Plymouth Rock. It is the place to renew the faith of the fathers in republican liberty. Plymouth was the immortal camping ground of a new march of the world, and she shall live in eternal memory, and forever be a place of pilgrimages.

She has marked the events of her heroic history clearly and well. Not only rises the Faith Monument over the town, the harbor, the graves, the Billington Sea, but a few miles away stands the pillarlike Standish Monument on Captain's Hill, an expression of strength in solitude worthy of the hero it commemorates.

Over the doors of Pilgrim Hall may be seen the allegory of the welcome of the Indians to the Pilgrims. In the hall are glorious paintings of incidents in Pilgrim history, which follow the original traditions. Here one may study the Standish sword; may find Elder Brewster's precious chair imprisoned in glass and iron, almost as great a treasure as the coronation stone of Westminster Abbey. Here in a side room may be seen the bones of the sachem of Nauset; we know not of any other remains of an Indian chief to be seen in New England. The kettle that was buried with the chief is placed in the case with his bones.

Here we may find the curious mortar and pestle of the

*National Monument to the Forefathers, at Plymouth, Massachusetts, erected 1859–1888.*

Winslow family, once used by Mistress Elizabeth Winslow, who adopted the little orphan Ellen More.

Go out and stand on the Rock under the granite canopy in whose chambers are precious relics; then go to the place where Elder Brewster's house stood, and drink from the spring that flowed when that good man was living. Stop on your way where the Common House stood. These places are all marked, and are near each other.

Then go to Billington Sea, two miles or more from the town through the woods. The so-called "sea" is a lovely lagoon with a wooded island. The oak leaves there are bright in summer, and the carpet of moss and evergreens under them will recall the times of the sagamores.

And, finally, stand on Burial Hill, and look out on the sheltered harbor where the Mayflower lay in the dreary winter of the great sickness, whose harvest was graves.

In Pilgrim Hall is the manuscript of a poem which caught the spirit of the great event of the Pilgrims' history. It was written by Felicia Hemans, set to music by her sister, Miss Browne (Mrs. Arkwright), and given to Sir Walter Scott to place for publication. It is said to have been composed one evening after tea, when Mrs. Hemans had been reading an account of the landing of the Pilgrim Fathers, in a paper sent to her by a brother in Canada. An autograph copy of the poem was secured by James T. Fields, and given in his will to the Pilgrim Society for Pilgrim Hall.

The picture of the landing of the Pilgrims in this poem is far from perfect; the coast is not "rock bound," nor did the Pilgrims keep "unstained" their "freedom to worship God"; but few poems ever more truly caught the spirit of an event. It is, and will probably ever be, the national hymn of Forefathers' Day. One may well repeat it when standing in view of the two monuments and of the solemn sea, and at no place more appropriately than at the graves of the precisioners and of their early descendants.

———

### THE LANDING OF THE PILGRIMS.

The breaking waves dashed high,
  On a stern and rock-bound coast,
And the woods against a stormy sky
  Their giant branches tossed.

And the heavy night hung dark,
  The hills and waters o'er,
When a band of exiles moored their bark
  On the wild New England shore.

Not as the conqueror comes,
  They, the true-hearted, came;
Not with the roll of stirring drums,
  And the trumpet that sings of fame;

Not as the flying come,
  In silence and in fear,
They shook the depths of the desert's gloom
  With their hymns of lofty cheer.

Amidst the storm they sang,
  And the stars heard, and the sea!
And the sounding aisles of the dim woods rang
  To the anthem of the free!

The ocean eagle soared
  From his nest by the white waves' foam,
And the rocking pines of the forest roared,
  This was their welcome home!

There were men with hoary hair
  Amidst that pilgrim band,
Why had they come to wither there,
  Away from their childhood's land?

There was woman's fearless eye,
  Lit by her deep love's truth;
There was manhood's brow, serenely high,
  And the fiery heart of youth.

What sought they thus afar?
  Bright jewels of the mine?
The wealth of seas? the spoils of war?
  They sought a faith's pure shrine!

Ay, call it holy ground,
  The soil where first they trod;
They have left unstained what there they found,
  Freedom to worship God!

17

## COMPACT DAY.

THE Pilgrim Fathers lived not for their own age alone, but for all time. They brought the free school with them in their purpose on the Mayflower. The schools of the nation celebrate many holidays, and they should add to the number Compact Day, November 11th, O. S. (22d, N. S.).

The principle of popular government was that day registered on the lid of William Brewster's chest, if the chest tradition be true, amid the children of the new nation. The Pilgrim Mothers, as well as the Pilgrim Fathers, may claim a thought of gratitude on that memorial day, and the children of the Mayflower may be recalled as the inspiration of these grand and worthy deeds, of which the past furnishes but few examples, which the future may not exceed.

The school is the foundation of national character. The republic must put its trust in the virtue of the people, and education must be the pillar of its strength.

The compact that was made for order in the Pilgrim republic, whose hall of legislation was a rocking ship in a desolate harbor, was to protect not only exiles, but the children of exiles, while education should produce men and generations of men, who should regard justice as more than position, welfare more than wealth, and virtue more than any other thing.

The Pilgrims came to the wilderness to found the school, to guard the school, and the school may well esteem it an honor and sacred trust to celebrate this purpose on Compact Day. On this day it will ever be a worthy thing to relate in some form the simple story of the children of the May-flower.

(11)